MW00570537

# More gunshots f◌
suddenly the acrid smell of gasoline
filled the air…

"They've hit our gas tank," Ian whispered urgently. "We've got to get as far away as we can before it blows."

He ushered Hope and Emi to the far side of the truck, then over a cement barrier. "Run for the trees," he said. He wrapped his arm around Hope, urging her on, but also shielding her with his body.

They were mere steps from the forest when the truck exploded. As they dived into a snowbank, burning pieces of the truck showered down all around them.

When Hope dared to lift her head, she knew she would never forget the sight of the truck full of burning Christmas trees lighting up the sky.

Ian pulled himself up beside her. "We have to keep moving. If we can get deep enough into the woods, we'll be able to get away."

Hope looked at him in disbelief. Getting away meant heading deep into the mountains in a blizzard, far from help…

**Cate Nolan** lives in New York City, but she escapes to the ocean any chance she gets. Once school is done for the day, Cate loves to leave her real life behind and play with the characters in her imagination. She's got that suspense-writer gene that sees danger and a story in everyday occurrences. Cate particularly loves to write stories of faith enabling ordinary people to overcome extraordinary danger. You can find her at www.catenolanauthor.com.

## Books by Cate Nolan

### Love Inspired Suspense

*Christmas in Hiding*
*Texas Witness Threat*
*Colorado Mountain Kidnapping*
*Colorado Christmas Survival*

Visit the Author Profile page at LoveInspired.com.

# Colorado Christmas Survival

## CATE NOLAN

**LOVE INSPIRED** SUSPENSE
INSPIRATIONAL ROMANCE

If you purchased this book without a cover you should be aware that this book is stolen property. It was reported as "unsold and destroyed" to the publisher, and neither the author nor the publisher has received any payment for this "stripped book."

# LOVE INSPIRED® SUSPENSE
## INSPIRATIONAL ROMANCE

ISBN-13: 978-1-335-98030-4

Colorado Christmas Survival

Copyright © 2024 by Mary Curry

All rights reserved. No part of this book may be used or reproduced in any manner whatsoever without written permission.

Without limiting the author's and publisher's exclusive rights, any unauthorized use of this publication to train generative artificial intelligence (AI) technologies is expressly prohibited.

This is a work of fiction. Names, characters, places and incidents are either the product of the author's imagination or are used fictitiously. Any resemblance to actual persons, living or dead, businesses, companies, events or locales is entirely coincidental.

For questions and comments about the quality of this book, please contact us at CustomerService@Harlequin.com.

® is a trademark of Harlequin Enterprises ULC.

Love Inspired
22 Adelaide St. West, 41st Floor
Toronto, Ontario M5H 4E3, Canada
www.LoveInspired.com

**Printed in Lithuania**

Recycling programs for this product may not exist in your area.

MIX
Paper | Supporting responsible forestry
FSC® C021394

Behold, a virgin shall be with child, and shall bring forth a son, and they shall call his name Emmanuel, which being interpreted is, God with us.
—*Matthew* 1:23

To Dana R. Lynn, Rhonda Starnes,
Belle Calhoune and Tina Radcliffe.

Writer friends are a precious gift,
and I am blessed by your friendship and support
over these many years. Thank you.

# ONE

"**K**nock, knock."

Hope Prescott looked up from her computer, smiled and called to her daughter, who was curled up on her office chair, face buried in a book. "Hey, Emi. Look who's here."

Emi kept her eyes glued to the page until Hope prompted her again. "Earth to Emi. You have a visitor."

Emi glanced up and her whole face transformed. "Uncle Steve!" The book went flying as she leaped from the cozy corner chair.

"Hey there, sweet girl." Steve scooped the seven-year-old blonde bookworm into his arms as if she weighed nothing. He turned to Hope. "Why are you still here? I told you to take the afternoon off."

"And I told you I had a marketing campaign that needed finishing touches."

"It can wait until after Christmas. Go. The rest of the gang left hours ago."

Hope rolled her eyes. "If you make me leave, I'll only take it home with me."

"Not this time." Steve pulled an envelope from his back pocket and handed it to Emi. The little girl opened the envelope and gasped.

"Christmas Village! You got us tickets?"

Hope ground her teeth and glared at her boss. He might

be her best friend in the world, but he had no right getting her child's hopes up over something impossible. "No room at the inn," she muttered.

Steve laughed and whispered into Emi's ear.

Hope's heart sank at the way her daughter's eyes lit up. She would have given anything to bring some Christmas joy into Emi's life, but by the time her daughter had discovered the best Christmas celebration in all of Colorado, everyone else in the state had snatched up the tickets along with every room in the small mountain town.

"Uncle Steve's friend has a ski chalet we can stay in. It's ours for…" Emi looked at Steve, who whispered in her ear again. Her eyes grew round. "Two weeks! We get two weeks at Christmas Village!"

Hope opened her mouth to protest, but Steve shook his head. "I won't hear another word about it. Emi deserves a special Christmas and who better to provide it than her favorite uncle?"

"Does that mean you're coming with us?"

A shadow passed over his dear face, confirming the feeling that had been nagging at Hope lately. Steve was keeping something from her.

Whatever it was, he shrugged it off. "Not this time. You need to get going before the storm blows in. Leave the computer here. Pack up your stuff. I want you on your way in—" he glanced down at his watch "—fifteen minutes."

There was no missing the underlying tension in his voice this time. Why was he so anxious for her to be gone? "Steve, what's wrong?"

He gave Emi a kiss, then set her down and stepped into the doorway. "We'll talk about it when you get back. No worries. Just go give your daughter the Christmas she needs. And if you really have to work, you can play along with Twelve Days 'til Christmas."

Hope stared at him as he disappeared into the hallway. Playing on their social media platform was not work. Her job was getting other people to play.

As Steve's footsteps receded down the hallway, Hope begrudgingly powered down her computer. He was right. She needed to set aside her work and focus on her daughter. Emi's childhood had been derailed by her father's death, and as much as Hope didn't want to think about her deceased husband and his betrayal, she couldn't deny the hole it had left in her daughter's life. So, she would shirk her workaholic ways and concentrate on Emi and Christm—

A piercing alarm shattered the air, cutting off her thoughts. Her phone dinged, and she grabbed it.

Intruder Alert: Exit Code 8

Hope's heart raced. Code 8 meant extreme danger and they were supposed to use the secret exits Steve had designed. But where was he? If they were alone in the building, she couldn't leave without him. Except she was supposed to. That was what they'd practiced.

She dashed across the room and peered down the hall. There was no sign of Steve, but in the distance she could hear the sound of running footsteps followed by a gunshot, and then silence. She slammed the door and engaged the safety latch.

"Mommy?"

The look of terror etched on her daughter's face galvanized Hope. Steve had been paranoid about a workplace attack. He'd made them practice escapes until the steps were drilled into their minds. She'd never expected to need to use them, but she knew what to do.

"Get our coats and backpacks." Her heart pounding, Hope pressed the panic button under her desk, which would ring at the sheriff's office. That was the fastest way to get help, though she hoped law enforcement had gotten the same alert she had. She shrugged on her coat, took the backpacks from Emi and grasped her hand before heading into a back passage that would open into the parking lot.

As she and Emi raced down the empty passageway, Hope's thoughts strayed to Steve and she whispered prayers for his safety. She listened for sirens and prayed law enforcement would get here fast, but as more gunshots echoed in the hallway, terror seized her heart and she feared it wouldn't be soon enough.

Hope punched in a special code that would deactivate the alarm on the door and eased it open. Snow was falling steadily as she poked her head out and looked around the quiet garden. All was peaceful and still back here, but her car was parked on the other side of the building—the side where all the shooting was coming from.

What should she do? She could try running away to wait for rescue, but Steve had built his tech complex in the middle of nowhere. With the storm blowing in, they risked death by exposure. She glanced down at Emi, who was huddling inside her coat—her bright pink coat. If anyone came looking for them, she'd stand out like a neon sign. Whipping off her own coat, Hope wrapped it around her daughter. She really had no choice but to try to get to her car.

"We have to be very quiet, baby," she whispered. "We're going to slide along the side of the building so no one looking out will see us."

Emi nodded, but her body was trembling. Hope couldn't tell if it was from cold or fear, but her heart broke for her baby girl. Worrying wouldn't get them to safety though. Holding on tight to Emi's hand, she began to sidle along the building. There were no windows on this back wall, so they were able to move quickly, but when they reached the corner, and Hope paused to take stock, she could hear voices. A shaft of light spread out from an open door.

"I don't see anyone out here. Maybe he was telling the truth that she left."

"Her car's still in the lot."

"Well, then where did she go?"

"If you hadn't hit him so hard, maybe we could have asked him."

Hope stifled a gasp as she listened to the argument. What had they done to Steve?

"Boss said to teach him a lesson."

The door slammed shut, and the voices faded away as Hope glanced down at Emi. If her daughter weren't here, she'd risk going back in to look for Steve, but her first concern had to be Emi's safety.

This side of the building housed the company cafeteria, and the walls were floor-to-ceiling glass. They were meant to be a relaxing way of bringing the outside in, part of the natural aesthetic Steve had created for his company. Most days, Hope appreciated the chance to bask in the sun while she had her lunch, but today all that glass was a hindrance to her escape.

"We're going to have to crawl along this wall—like inchworms," she teased, trying to make Emi relax. "I'll go first and you follow right behind my heels, okay?"

Emi shivered and silently fell to her knees. Hope dropped down in front of her and began to inch her way along the wall. The lunchroom had never felt as big as it did while she made slow progress through the drifts that were still piled up from last week's storm. When they finally reached the end, Hope peered around the edge and her heart sank.

Steve's motorcycle was parked in his spot by the front

door, and an unfamiliar truck, presumably belonging to the gunman, was idling in the walkway. Her car sat alone in the lot, spotlighted by the glow of the lights.

*Where was the sheriff? Why hadn't anyone responded yet?*

Another round of gunfire echoed from inside the building and terror spurred Hope onward. "We have to run as fast as you can, Emi. I'll open the door and you jump in and get your seat belt on yourself, okay?"

Again, Emi gave a silent nod.

Hope fumbled in her pocket for her key fob. "One, two, three, run," she whispered, and the two of them dashed across the parking lot. Fearful that the sound might be overheard, she waited until they were crouched behind the car to push the button on her fob. As soon as the car beeped and the door was unlatched, she helped Emi in and closed the door securely. If only she could assure her daughter's safety that easily.

By the time Hope had opened the front door and settled in her own seat with the key in the ignition, she could hear shouts from the front of the building.

She quickly turned the key and shifted into gear as gunfire erupted behind her. "Stay down low, Emi," Hope warned as she lead-footed the accelerator.

The car shot forward, tires spinning on snow that had begun to accumulate in the lot. She fishtailed as she shot around the corner, but the back tires caught and she was able to straighten out and speed down the long snowy road that led out to the highway.

"Mommy, I'm scared."

*I am, too.* Hope didn't say the words aloud, but her white-knuckled grip on the steering wheel betrayed her terror as she drove up the entrance ramp to Highway 160.

The Colorado highway could be a snowy death trap, so

she didn't dare take her eyes off the road or her hands off the wheel, but she needed to reassure her daughter. "It will be okay, Emi. We trust Jesus to protect us."

Hope smiled despite her fear as she heard Emi begin to murmur prayers. Echoing her daughter, she whispered the words beneath her breath, alternating them with "Jesus, take the wheel" as she stared through her rearview mirror into the swirling world of white—and saw headlights appear behind them.

There was a chance it was nothing, just fellow travelers in a storm. But she'd seen no other vehicles in either direction since leaving the parking lot. Anyone with sense was safe at home. She tried to focus on prayer, but fear settled in her heart.

The headlights grew brighter, and her fingers clenched the steering wheel. The truck was traveling too fast for the road conditions.

She glanced back, panicked as the vehicle behind closed the distance between them, but with road conditions deteriorating, she couldn't go any faster. She cast another look in her mirror, and terror washed over her at the sight of a gun protruding from the passenger window. "Emi, head down!"

The back windshield exploded.

"Mommy!" Emi screamed.

Another gunshot and Hope swallowed her own scream. The truck drew closer until she felt it slam her back bumper. She pressed her accelerator to the floor, but it did no good as the truck sped up and rammed her from behind.

He was trying to drive her off the road! As she struggled for control of the car, Hope crouched over the wheel, trying to see ahead on the curving road. Her wipers couldn't keep up with the heavy snow, but as they cleared a swath, there was no missing the blinding headlights of an approaching eighteen-wheeler.

The vehicle behind revved and shot forward. Hope prayed and swung the wheel with all her might as the hard hit sent her skidding across the highway directly into the path of the oncoming headlights.

*Jesus, I trust in you. Please help us.*

Ian Fraser rubbed his brow, fighting the eye fatigue that came with trying to see through driving snow. He should have stopped at the last rest stop and waited out the storm, but something had urged him to keep going. Maybe it was knowing the local veterans' center was counting on his truckful of Christmas trees for their annual fundraiser. Maybe it was wanting to be safe at the ranch in this ferocious storm. Or maybe he was just hungry. Whatever the reason, he'd kept going, and there was no use regretting it now. He had enough regrets in his life. No need to add new ones.

Keeping one hand steady on the wheel, he stretched, trying to ease the kink in his neck, but the sudden glare of headlights ahead caught his full attention.

And gunshots. Who was foolish enough to be firing guns in this weather? They could set off an avalanche that would close down the whole highway.

Ian pumped the brakes to slow his rig, but the car in the other lane was flying toward him at an alarming speed. The driver appeared to turn, but Ian watched as the car spun helplessly out of control right into his path. He grasped the wheel tightly and swung his own rig to the left, barely missing contact with the car and the truck that had been traveling behind it.

Ian slowed his truck to a halt and quickly hopped down. There was no way that driver had been able to avoid crashing and he could only hope they'd managed to find a soft drift.

Wind whipped stinging bites of snow into his face as he trudged through the rapidly accumulating snow.

"Hello," he called. "Anyone there?"

The gusts scattered his words, so he cupped his hands to his mouth and tried again. There was still no response, but that didn't satisfy his concerns. If the people were injured, they might be unable to answer.

Doubling over in his fight against the wind, Ian scoured the sides of the road, looking for where the car had gone over the side. Praise the Lord, it had been here rather than farther up the pass where the mountainside dropped off beside the road.

After a few minutes of searching, he found where the car had plowed headfirst into a deep drift. The doors stood open, and two men in balaclavas were searching around the outside.

"You all right over there?" Ian called.

The men looked up, and Ian thought he must be imagining the irritation on their faces.

"Just looking to help out whoever crashed here," one of them called back.

They seemed to confer a moment before one headed in his direction. "Looks like there was a woman and a child in the car. They must have been ejected. We're searching down below. Can you set up flares on the road?"

"Sure thing," Ian answered. "Did you call for help or should I?"

"My buddy called it in."

Ian turned to get the flares from his truck, but instinct that had served him well through multiple tours in Afghanistan made him turn back just in time to ward off a blow to the back of his head. The gun glanced off his temple instead. That same instinct sent him to his knees pretending to be struck. He stilled his breathing and waited, ready to spring if the man attacked again, but he seemed to be satisfied and headed off downhill, calling to his friend to hurry.

Ian lay in the snow, waiting until he was sure the man was out of sight before he rose to his knees. His temple ached, but he knew God had been looking out for him. Another few inches and he'd be dead. What had he stumbled into?

Suddenly he wondered about the car he'd seen go off the road. Had that been an accident? Or had these men had something to do with it? And who were the missing occupants of the car?

He was all about helping people in need, but Ian was outnumbered and outgunned here. The best thing he could do was get back to his truck and make that call to highway patrol.

Not wanting to draw their attention, Ian crawled his way through the snow until he reached the side of the road. He rose cautiously, but there was no sign of the men, so he hurried across to where he'd left his truck. As he reached the cab, he noticed a piece of pink fuzz caught in the driver's side door. He glanced back quickly to see if either of the men had followed him, but there was still no sign of them. They were too busy searching for people who, he suspected, were hiding in his truck. He pocketed the fuzz, opened the door and quickly climbed up, pulling the door shut behind him.

The moment he settled in his seat, Ian knew his suspicions were correct. The woman and child had taken refuge in his truck. He sensed their presence, and the summery scent of lavender tickled his nose in confirmation.

He started the ignition and shifted the truck into gear. "I know you're there. Give me one good reason I should trust you over them."

# TWO

"The blood frozen to your temple might be a good one."

Ian reached up and touched the side of his head. When his hand came away sticky, he simply nodded and put the truck in gear. "Where are you headed?"

There was silence for a long moment before he heard her soft reply. "Anywhere you're going is fine, as long as it's away from them."

Ian turned his attention to the road and started driving. All thoughts of waiting out the storm had vanished the moment he'd spied that pink fuzz, but the driving conditions were steadily deteriorating. Snow was piling up faster than plows could keep up. He had chains on his tires, as required by state law, so he was less worried about spinning out than he was about visibility. If they took it slowly, all should be well.

But would they be able to take it slowly? Ian glanced in his side-view mirror. Would the men continue searching the area where her car had gone off the road, or would they soon be on his tail? Driving Highway 160 required concentration in the best of times, but this stretch ahead was particularly perilous.

He should radio for help, but first he needed to know what he was dealing with. At the moment, he had nothing more to go on than two huddled figures and a piece of pink fluff. He'd heard from the men with guns. Now he needed to hear from his stowaways.

"You can come out now."

Silence from the back seat only amplified the howling of the wind and the rhythmic slap of his tire chains against the road.

Ian blew out a soft breath and tried again. "I'm sure you're scared, but you're safe with me. My name is Ian. I'm a rancher. I saw you go off the road and just tried to help." He touched the tender side of his head and chuckled softly. "And got a pretty nice headache as a result."

"I'm sorry."

The voice sounded genuinely remorseful, which made Ian feel a little better about his choice to drive off with strangers in his truck. He was trusting his instincts here, that anyone who had been running from those men must be in trouble.

"Okay, whenever you're ready. But this storm is only getting worse, and it would be a big help if I knew what we're up against."

"Thank you."

Ian strained to catch her words over the raging storm. "I could hear better if you would come up here and talk with me. There's no sign of your pursuers," he added as reassurance.

"They'll be back."

The defeated tone of her voice nearly undid him. "Then come tell me about them so I'm prepared."

He could hear some shifting around followed by whispers before the curtain parted and a woman emerged between the seats. Ian reached out a hand to steady her against the roll of the truck, but she flinched away and slid into the passenger seat.

He risked a quick glance, just long enough to observe her huddled inside a heavy winter coat. A faux-fur-trimmed hood obscured most of her face, but as she turned to face him, he noted stray whisps of blond hair framing delicate features. He felt her studying him in return, so he waited, allowing her time to feel at ease.

"Whenever you're ready, tell me what happened."

She tilted her head toward the back seat, and gave a subtle shake. Ian only caught the motion out of the corner of his eye, but he understood her meaning. Whatever she needed to say, she didn't want the person back there to hear. Because it was a child or for some other reason? He reached over and turned on the radio, flipping through stations until he found one that was playing popular Christmas music. He flipped another switch to raise the volume on the back speakers while he lowered the sound in the front.

"Thank you." She paused before continuing. "If you're really a rancher, why are you driving a truck full of trees in a blizzard?"

Ian chuckled. "I guess that does seem odd." Maybe if he offered some information about himself, she'd be more at ease. "My parents own a ranch that's been in the family for generations. My brother, my sister and I each have our own acreage to do what we want with. When I got out of the army, I decided to try my hand at growing Christmas trees. This truckful is headed toward a veterans' center for a fundraiser."

"That's really generous."

He smiled again, but this time it was more forced. "I do what I can to help. Now, have I answered enough questions? Are you ready to tell me the story?" He felt her hesitation. "I can't keep you safe if I don't know who they are and what they want."

"That's just the problem. I don't know who they are."

Ian stared into the swirling snow and considered her answer. It was interesting for what she'd left out. "But you know what they want?"

"Not really."

From his years as an Army Ranger, Ian had plenty of experience in knowing when to wait and when to coax for information. This seemed a time to wait. He focused on the road ahead, but he was acutely aware of the tension radiating off the woman sitting in his passenger seat. She was nervously fingering her gloves, and he sensed she was trying to decide what she should say.

He also caught her frequent glances toward the side-view mirror.

A glare of headlights from a snowplow in the oncoming lane made Ian shield his eyes to see better, but she reacted more dramatically, sliding down in the seat until she was below the dashboard level. Whoever those men were, they clearly had her terrified.

She wedged herself into the corner against the door and folded her arms across her chest in a gesture that came across as more defensive than defiant.

"I don't know who they are, but they invaded my workplace late this afternoon. I would assume it has something to do with that break-in. But my daughter and I got away, and they've been chasing us ever since. I don't understand that part. If there was something they wanted, wouldn't you think it would be back there?"

Ian wasn't sure what he'd been expecting, but it wasn't that. He needed more details, but at least it was a start. If she was being truthful, he'd learned two important facts. She was innocent, and the men pursuing her were extremely dangerous. No surprise there.

"Have you reported it?"

"No, but a safety alert went out, so the sheriff's office should have gotten that, and I hit the panic button on my desk before we fled."

"What kind of company do you work for that has such fancy security?"

"It's a tech company, but we design apps and social media platforms, nothing that should have triggered something like this."

Ian thought back to the two men who had attacked him. That did seem sort of extreme for something having to do with social media unless it was corporate espionage. But why attack…? "What's your name?"

She hesitated just long enough to warrant suspicion, but he got that she was scared. "I already told you my name. Ian Fraser. Do you want me to call the sheriff?"

"Please."

"Then I'll need a location and some more details. And your name."

She gave him the address.

"Whoa. They've been chasing you that far?"

She nodded, and a whimper escaped her lips. He was beginning to understand the depth of her fear. "Was there anyone else there?"

"I don't think so. Steve, he's my boss, he was in my office just before they burst in. He said everyone else had left."

"Why were you there?"

She hiccuped, and he realized she was trying to hold back sobs. "You sound like Steve. He asked me the same thing right before he…"

Her voice trailed off, so Ian prompted. "Right before he what?"

"Right before he gave Emi a Christmas present and said he was sending us on vacation for two weeks."

"Emi is your daughter?"

She glanced at the back seat again before answering. "Yes."

"Why was your boss sending you on vacation?"

She turned her body so she was facing Ian directly now. "It was a Christmas present for Emi. He's been looking out for her ever since...ever since..."

Her voice faltered, so Ian gave her a moment before asking, "Ever since what?"

She cleared her throat and again spoke softly. "Ever since my husband died."

This was like playing a game of twenty questions, but instead of getting closer to the solution, each response opened up more questions.

Even across the cab, Ian felt the shudders that suddenly wracked her body. Remembering how she'd flinched when he'd tried to steady her, Ian took his cue. She was too skittish for him to extend a comforting hand, so he tried to calm her with his voice.

"Take your time. Do you need a tissue? There should be a box under the seat."

He waited while she located the tissues and wiped her tears.

She looked in the back seat. "Emi?"

There was no response, and she visibly relaxed, but her voice was lower when she continued.

"I think she's asleep."

She took another moment to get her emotions under control, and Ian used the time to carefully study the road behind him. Still no sign of any other vehicle. Actually, there was a surprising lack of traffic, even allowing for the road conditions. With the storm worsening, they'd probably close off the pass at the foot of the mountain.

"Steve came to give Emi her present," she continued. "He told us to leave, and then he headed back to his office." She took a deep breath. "I heard shouts and then gunshots, and then someone running in the hallway."

She shivered at the memory, but her voice assumed a matter-of-fact tone that he took as a means of getting herself through the retelling as she detailed their escape. Ian still couldn't believe that this brave woman had managed to escape gunmen on a treacherous highway in a blizzard.

"I've got enough to call it in now," he assured her. "But I still need your name."

She didn't respond immediately, but Ian understood her hesitation. She didn't know him as anyone more than the driver of the truck she'd hidden inside of in a desperate move to escape men trying to kill her. In her position, he'd be hesitant too.

He wished there was something he could do to reassure her that she was safe with him, but only kindness and time would accomplish that. "There's water in the box where you found the tissues if you'd like something to drink," he offered. "Sorry I don't have something hot."

"Thank you," she murmured. "Hope. That's my name."

Ian decided against pressing for a last name. "Thanks for trusting me, Hope."

There was usually reliable cell service along this stretch due to the tower at the top of Wolf Creek Pass, so he opted to call 911 rather than use the truck's CB radio. He identified himself, established their location and relayed what he knew.

The operator took the information and his contact details. She promised that law enforcement was dispatched to the crime scene, but there wasn't much she could offer him in terms of support on the road. Multiple-vehicle accidents had traffic backed up in both directions across the pass, and emergency responders had their hands full. She promised to let him know as soon as help was available, but Ian caught the tension in her voice and the unspoken reality. They were on their own, trapped on a mountain pass with potential killers.

It wasn't good news. Hope could tell from the slump of Ian's shoulders as he listened to the operator. She hadn't really expected anything different. People had warned her against traveling across Wolf Creek Pass, but she'd never planned to do it in a storm, much less with men chasing her.

She opened the water bottle, listening for the crack of the seal and mourning the circumstances that made her be suspicious of a man who was clearly trying to help. Without her, he would be delivering his trees and heading home. Instead, he was risking his life to protect a woman and child he knew nothing about. She owed him a measure of trust for that.

Ian disconnected the call and glanced over at her. "She said the sheriff was dispatched, but I got the sense he was already there. She took my contact information and said she'd let us know."

"Thank you."

"But we're going to have to wait on getting help out here. Apparently there are accidents on both sides of the pass."

"Beware the wolf."

He threw her a look.

"Beware the wolf. That's what all the signs say. The ones warning you to take it slow over Wolf Creek Pass."

Ian nodded. "I've driven it many times. You're right.

You do have to take it slow. Not like we have much choice in this weather."

Hope stared at the near whiteout conditions and whispered a prayer of gratitude that the man was able to keep a sense of humor even under such dire conditions. "I'm sorry you got caught up in this. I shouldn't have hidden in your truck."

"Why did you?"

She shrugged as she thought about it. "I didn't know what else to do. When they ran us off the road, I knew it was only by the grace of God that you managed to avoid hitting us. I also knew they wouldn't give up since they'd followed me that far. I was going to try to cross the highway and take shelter under the trees until help could come." She shivered at the memory. "But then the wind blew your door open." She paused and sighed.

"I'd been praying for rescue. Your truck…it felt like an answer to my prayers. At that moment, I wasn't thinking that doing it would put you in danger."

She could see a smile curl his lips as he began to speak.

"I'm not sure anyone has ever considered me an answer to their prayers before."

Some instinct made her tease him back. "I said your truck."

Ian threw back his head and laughed. "Touché."

"There's no need for regrets. It was the right decision," he continued quietly when the laughter had drifted off. "You and Emi could have frozen to death waiting on rescue."

Unspoken, the words *if the gunmen hadn't gotten you first* hung between them.

"We have a long, slow drive down the mountain. You can rest if you want."

Hope turned toward the window. Huddled inside her jacket she pretended, but she knew she wouldn't sleep, and she knew she wasn't fooling him. Too many thoughts spun through her head in a dizzying whirl.

As much as she wanted to forget what she'd seen, she had to try to remember the details.

She owed that much and more to Steve. He'd been her best friend since sophomore year of college. It was almost a cliché. He and Keith had been the computer geeks she'd met when her laptop died in the midst of a research paper deadline. They'd fixed her computer and saved her 4.0 GPA. In return she'd kept them supplied with cookies. Years later, when Keith had betrayed her and she'd been a widowed single mother, Steve had rescued her again, giving her this job and drawing her back into life.

She'd repaid him with more than cookies that time. The app he'd designed was incredibly clever, but he'd had no clue what to do with it. Her marketing expertise provided the solution, and before long, Twelve Days 'til Christmas was climbing the charts across all platforms. She was still stunned at the success of the campaign that had left them all financially independent. It had been the perfect collaboration of Steve's technological brilliance and her marketing savvy. They'd been riding an incredible high.

Until today.

Tears rolled down her cheek unchecked. "I need to call the hospital and check on my friend."

"You can try, but they probably won't release info if you're not next of kin."

Hope sighed as she looked up the number and called the county hospital. She was essentially the closest thing he had to kin other than his admin, Helen.

As Ian had predicted, the hospital refused to even tell

her if Steve was a patient. Next she tried Helen, but that call went straight to voicemail.

She didn't know what to do now, where to turn. She couldn't continue to rely on the kindness of a stranger. Once they made it off the mountain, she would be on her own, responsible for protecting Emi against men who what... wanted her dead?

"Do you think you would recognize their truck?"

Ian's voice had an edge to it that jolted Hope from her misery.

"Take a look at the side mirror, and see what you think."

Hope reached for the crumpled tissue she'd dropped in her lap and rubbed the tears from her eyes. "The mirror is covered with snow."

Ian pressed a button to lower the window, and she used her jacket sleeve to clear the snow and ice. Her heart sank as a familiar silhouette materialized. For a brief moment, she wanted to close the window, let the snow build up again and pretend she'd never seen the truck. Fatigue crashed through her as she turned to Ian instead.

"It's them. They've caught up."

# THREE

Defeat was back in Hope's voice. After hearing the details of what she'd endured, Ian understood why, and on a personal level, he wanted—*needed*—to help. Something deep within his protective nature was triggered by the sight of that truck bearing down on them. It hardened his resolve to do whatever was necessary to keep this woman and child safe. "Not yet they haven't," he promised. "We're not giving up so easily."

Hope turned from the window. Her shoulders were slumped, and she seemed to want to disappear inside her jacket. Obviously, she didn't share his confidence. Understandable. She was exhausted and probably hungry, and she had to be absolutely terrified.

"They have guns, a fast truck and apparently a strong motive to catch me...or kill me."

Ian winked at her. "You have me."

Hope choked on a laugh. Not exactly the reaction he'd intended, but if it helped defuse her anxiety, all the better. "I'm not joking. I know it sounds egotistical, but I'm a trained Army Ranger, and I know these mountain roads."

"What are we going to do?"

Ian didn't respond immediately. The actual answer was that he wouldn't know until the men made their move, but he doubted that would instill confidence.

"The first thing we need to do is make sure everyone is secure. You should go in the back with Emi."

"But—"

"It will be easier for me to focus if I know you're not a visible target. There are seat restraints, and you'll find extra blankets and pillows in the cabinet that you can use as protective cushioning. Make sure you're both belted in. This might get rough."

Hope rose without a word, though he could see she was biting down hard on her lip. The truck lurched as a sudden gust of wind caught the Christmas trees lashed in the back. This time she was the one who grasped his arm to steady herself, and Ian felt her soft touch straight to his heart.

"It'll be okay," he said gently.

She nodded bravely and stepped into the back.

"Mommy?"

Emi's frightened voice cracked his heart.

"It's okay, love," She echoed his promise. "This is Ian, and he's going to keep us safe."

Ian's heart swelled at the ring of trust in Hope's voice. She was probably forcing it for the sake of her daughter, but he still took the responsibility of her trust seriously.

He cast a glance out the window. Snow was coating his mirror, but he could see well enough to realize the gap between the trucks was down to a car length now. He needed Hope to get settled fast.

"Hi, Emi. Your mom is going to build you a pillow fort because the road is getting bumpy really fast." He put emphasis on the word *fast*. He didn't want to alarm Emi, but Hope needed to know they were running out of time. "Closing in, Hope."

"Gotcha."

He heard the cabinet door slam, and within minutes, she confirmed their status. "We're belted in."

Ian nodded acknowledgment and then forced himself to shut out the soothing sound of Hope's voice as she comforted her daughter. Likewise, he shoved aside his anger at the men who were trying to harm them. He needed a clear mind and full concentration on the road ahead and the men in the truck.

Snow was piling up in drifts along the side of the highway, nearly to the top of the mile markers, but Ian had driven this route enough to know every landmark, every twist and turn. He was banking on two things—their pursuers lacking his familiarity and their being focused more on his truck and the people within than on the road itself.

A sudden jolt interrupted his thoughts. Were they serious? They were going to try to run him off the road with a truck a quarter his size?

Ian rolled down his window to clear the snow off his mirror, and suddenly their plan made sense. A shotgun was protruding from the passenger window of the truck.

He wasn't particularly worried about them hitting Emi or Hope because there was no window in the back of the cab, but taking him out would cause a crash that would likely kill them too.

His vow of protection suddenly took on more urgency. "Hang on."

Two could play this game. Ian floored the accelerator, murmuring a prayer that the chains would let him keep traction on the snow-covered road. As the truck picked up speed, he swung hard to the left, cutting off the other truck and sending it skidding across the road. He eased off the gas and gently swung back into his lane.

"Everybody okay back there?"

"So far."

"I'm going to try to put some distance between us, but I'm sure they're not giving up." Ian kept a wary eye on his mirrors as he focused on the road. His truck was now almost to the most treacherous section of the pass, so he had to downshift and feather his brakes—not so easy on a snowy road. He hoped he'd put the killers out of commission long enough that he could make it to a flat stretch, but he wasn't counting on it.

Five minutes of driving proved him right. The one thing he had going for him was the lack of traffic in either direction, but that meant that the headlights currently reflected in his mirror belonged to the enemy. This was not the place he wanted to encounter them. Two quick switchbacks made traveling this road concerning in good conditions, dangerous in bad weather and potentially deadly with someone trying to force you off the side.

He had a plan in mind and, though it wasn't ideal, it should work. He didn't want to worry Hope, but he needed to warn her.

"Company is gaining on us again, but I know how to handle them. Just up ahead, we'll be coming to the first of two runaway truck ramps."

"That sounds... terrifying."

Ian grimaced. "Not as bad as the alternative. This descent is very steep, and there's a hairpin turn ahead. Sometimes trucks lose their brakes or are heading down too fast to make the turns. The ramps are a way of slowing down rather than crashing."

"How's that going to help us?"

"The signs are covered in snow right now, but I know where the first ramp is. I'm going to build up speed heading into it, but I'll wait until the last minute to make the turn up the ramp. Hopefully, they'll speed on by."

"We'll be praying, right Emi?"

Ian listened to the sweet sound of their voices joined in prayer and calm settled over him.

It was a risky plan that required careful timing for everything to go right. He had to avoid letting the other truck catch him too soon, increasing speed enough to fool them but not enough to risk overshooting the ramp.

All in near whiteout conditions on the side of a mountain.

Ian joined his voice to theirs. "Lord, help us."

Minutes dragged by as he carefully watched the road. The other truck was gaining on him, slowly pulling within firing range. Ian alternated between watching them in his mirror and keeping alert for the ramp.

The first gunshot felt like it ripped through him, though there was no indication the truck had been hit. A second shot pinged off the back of his cab. *Please Lord, let this ramp appear.*

At last, as they came around a curve, he recognized the landmarks. On his right, walls of sheer rock rose straight up from the road, but on the left, the land sloped down. Time to accelerate. There would be one more curve. He had to lead them into it before veering sharply right and up the ramp. Eyes intent on the road, Ian recognized the arch of the snow-covered sign overhanging the road.

He accelerated again and watched in the side mirror to be sure his pursuers were following. When they increased speed as well, he angled the truck toward the ramp and hit the gas hard at the same moment he doused his lights. The truck headed up the ramp in darkness, and Ian held his breath until he saw the lights of the other truck fade around the corner and out of sight.

He quickly eased off the gas, downshifted and let the

ramp do its job. Slowly, the large truck lost momentum, until it came to a standstill three-fourths of the way up the ramp. Ian bowed his head in a prayer of thanksgiving.

"That was—"

"Terrifying. I know. I'm sorry."

"Amazing," Hope replied.

Ian huffed grimly. "Well, if you enjoyed that, I'm sure there's more to come."

Hope knew he was right. Once the men realized the truck was no longer ahead of them, they'd circle back. Her body started to tremble. What did they want with her?

"Mommy, you're shaking."

"I am. You know how scared I get when we go on the roller coaster? This is a little like that, isn't it? Imagine riding a roller coaster in the snow!"

While Emi contemplated the fun in that, Hope spoke to Ian. "Now what? Are we stuck here?" What had seemed like an ingenious plan suddenly left her feeling like they were sitting ducks.

"Under normal circumstances, we'd contact highway patrol and pay to get towed out, but we can't wait for that. I'm going to try to back down."

Heart in her throat, Hope felt like she was holding her breath for a lifetime as he ever so slowly eased the big rig back down the ramp. She didn't think she imagined Ian's weary exhale when they finally leveled out on the highway and were facing forward. "Any sign of our friends?"

"Not yet."

Ian's tense reply matched her own feelings, so she bit back her next question. He sensed it and answered anyway. "I'd prefer to turn around and head back, but that won't stop them from finding us again. We have to keep moving forward. It's not a good solution, but it's the best we have."

Hope recognized the same resignation in his voice that she'd felt when she chose to climb in a stranger's truck. When you were trapped with killers on a long stretch of mountainous highway in a blizzard, your options were severely limited.

"The most treacherous turn is in about two miles. If we can avoid them until that, there's a turnoff to a campground not much farther along. We can hide out there."

"And if we can't?"

"Let's just pray that we can."

There was a lot of room for something to go wrong in Ian's plan, but he was right. They could only pray it went right.

For a mile or so it did. Hope thought she might go mad from the tension and the inability to see what was happening. She agreed with Ian that she needed to be back here with Emi, out of the line of fire, but that meant she had no way of knowing what was happening. She didn't like not being in control of her own life. Since her husband's death four years earlier, she'd been responsible for every life decision for herself and Emi. Now, at the most critical moment she'd ever faced, it was clear how very little control she really did have. She had to give it up to God…but that was much easier said than done. Especially with men shooting at you.

Hope didn't have to be in the front seat to see the sudden glare of headlights, nor did she need to hear Ian's frustrated groan to know who was driving the truck heading straight at them.

Shots rang out, and the front windshield exploded.

Hope tried to muffle her scream, but it was too late. Emi launched herself into her mother's arms and clung tight.

"Ian?" Hope waited desperately to hear his voice, to be assured he hadn't been hit. She couldn't live with herself if he came to harm because of her.

"All in one piece," he responded. "The same can't be said for the windshield."

Hope peered through the gap between the seats and gasped at the shattered glass. The windshield looked like a massive spiderweb.

"Hope, I'm going to need your help. I have to break through a section of the glass, or I won't be able to keep driving. There's a toolbox wedged behind my seat. I need the hammer and a blanket. I can't stop here, so you'll have to come hold the wheel steady while I smash through the glass."

He had to be joking. Her hands were shaking so hard, there was no chance she could hold a bicycle steady, let alone the wheel of a truck full of Christmas trees. But if he could do all this for her... Hope took a deep breath and steeled herself to do what was necessary. After retrieving the hammer and blanket, she braced herself against the back of his seat.

"You can do this," he encouraged her. "Just slide into the seat as I stand up. Both hands on the wheel and hold tight. It's no different than steering your car."

He eased around her, and while she clung to the wheel, holding on with all her might, he used the blanket to cover the windshield and pounded the glass with the hammer. She flinched at the sound of glass splintering, but then it was over, and Ian was congratulating her on a job well done.

He shoved the blanket full of glass into the well under the dash and then guided her up, still holding the wheel as he slipped back into his seat. Hope slid over into the passenger seat, feeling like a giant rag doll, completely spent but waiting to see what happened next.

"It's snowing inside the truck!"

Emi's excitement was amusing, but it didn't take more than a moment to realize Ian couldn't continue to drive like this. Wind was gusting snow through the broken glass, reducing visibility almost as badly as the webbed glass had. "We have to get off the road, don't we?"

Ian nodded. "I was hoping that would work, but the storm is too powerful. Our last chance is the second runaway truck ramp." Tension thrummed in his voice. "This one won't be as easy as the other. Think of it more as a rocket launch compared to your last roller coaster."

Hope's stomach dropped.

"It's going to be harder for me to get up the ramp with visibility so low. Can you see out your corner of the windshield?"

Hope realized that the shatter hadn't spread to the right of the passenger side. She pulled herself up to the window and peered through her section of glass. Snow was starting to build up now that the wipers couldn't work, but she could still see the road. "What am I looking for?"

"Make sure we're not too close to the rocks. See if you can tell if I'm centered in the lane."

While Ian tried to swat the snow out of his face, Hope squinted into the dim path cut by their headlights. "It will be easier to see if I lower my window." She pressed the switch, and as the window slowly rolled down, she saw exactly what he meant by rocks. Right outside her window was a wall of rock so close she could reach out and touch it. "You need to move more to the left or we're going to scrape into the rocks."

Hope watched with bated breath as the truck slowly eased away from the wall. The flatbed section fishtailed just enough that she felt the jolt as the trees brushed along the rocks.

Now that she had space, she leaned her head out the window. "I can see the ramp up ahead. If you keep going straight, you'll hit it right on center."

"Make sure you're belted in," Ian warned. "This ramp is steep."

Hope pulled her head in just as she noticed headlights reflecting off her mirror. She reached to secure her belt. "They're back," she murmured.

"I see." Ian shook his head as if to clear his thoughts. "Let's focus one step at a time. If I try to head down this road, unable to see, we'll go off the cliff at the curve. This ramp is our only chance. We'll worry about them once we've stopped."

Hope swallowed hard. It took everything she had not to melt into total panic, but he was right. Keeping a cool head and taking the challenges one at a time was the only way through this. But she'd be praying the whole time.

"Don't put your head out again. We can't risk them taking a shot at you. Whatever guidance you can give through your corner of the windshield will be help enough."

Once again, Hope bent toward the glass. Ahead, the ramp rose before them. So much snow covered the lane that it was difficult to see where the road ended. Only when the gusts blew could she see the black-and-gold-striped posts edging the side. Hopefully, Ian had similar ones he could see out his side window. The truck hit the base of the ramp, but it didn't take long to realize they didn't have enough momentum to make it. Against all logic, Ian pressed down on the accelerator, hoping to get even a little farther up and away from the truck bearing down on them again.

A gunshot sounded, and his side mirror shattered into pieces. Emi's whimper cut to Hope's heart, but it was too late to move back to her now. If they had even a prayer of surviving, Ian needed her up here guiding him.

A barrage of gunfire erupted, and suddenly the truck shifted.

"I think they got a tire," Ian muttered. He held tight to the wheel, but Hope could feel the change in traction. The truck started to slide and tilted heavily toward the left. Now it was Hope who wanted to whimper. *Please Lord, have mercy.*

"We have to get out, Hope."

She nodded. It was obvious they were no longer safe in the cab. "How?"

The truck gave another lurch and gravity took hold.

"Hang on, we're going over."

Hope's heart stuttered in terror as she gripped the roof hold. "Emi," she cried. "Hold tight to the harness."

"Mommy, I'm so scared."

"It'll be okay, baby. As soon as the truck settles, we'll climb out." She forced a reassuring tone, but her mind was racing a mile a minute thinking of the terrifying danger ahead.

Wind howled down the ramp. The truck sounded like it was coming apart at the seams, and with a final shudder, the cab twisted, landing on the passenger side. The gunfire had ceased momentarily, but that was almost more frightening. What were the men doing?

Ian groaned, and Hope realized he had landed hard with his arm twisted under him. Before she could ask him about it, he was struggling to unharness his seat belt.

"Are you okay?" he queried.

"Yes. Emi?"

There was no answer, so Hope unsnapped her belt and dove between the seats. Emi was curled in a ball in the corner, tears streaming down her face. "Are you hurt, baby?"

Emi shook her head, but she couldn't get any words out.

While she'd been checking on her daughter, Ian had been trying to force the driver's door open. As soon as he got it unstuck, he gave it a shove upright.

Immediately the door was riddled with bullets.

Hope screamed. At this point, she didn't care who heard. The men were sitting out there just waiting to shoot them as they emerged from the truck.

Ian crawled into the backseat with them. "Be very quiet," he whispered. "I think they've gone along the road so they're parallel to us. We're going to go out through the windshield and climb around the side of the cab away from them."

He raised the lid on the bench Emi had been sitting on and pulled out some tarps. "We'll wrap these around us as protection from the glass, and then surf down the side. Can you do that?"

Roller coasters, surfing. Hope was beside herself, but she would try anything that gave her a chance at escaping the killers. She nodded and reached for one of the tarps. "I'm taking Emi with me." She grabbed their backpacks and strapped them to her chest.

Ian ripped the harness loose from the bench and quickly used it to attach Emi to Hope's back. Then he wrapped the tarp tightly around them and guided them back to the front seat. "I'm going to lift you through the window."

"But your arm—"

"Don't worry about my arm. Just slide down the truck, keep low and wait for me. I'll be right behind you."

Hope held the tarp tightly closed as Ian pushed her through the glass. She could hear the moan he tried to muffle. The man was in serious pain, but there was nothing she could do to help him until they were free.

Gunshots still sounded around them, but she ignored the sound and focused on her assignment. Once they had cleared the windshield, she flattened herself and surfed down the cab of the truck. She landed softly in a drift of snow and whispered to Emi to stay quiet. Moments later, Ian landed beside them.

More gunshots followed, and suddenly the acrid smell of diesel filled the air.

"They've hit the fuel tank," Ian whispered urgently. "We've got to get as far away as we can before it blows."

He ushered them to the far side of the truck and over a cement barrier. "Run for the trees," he urged.

If it was a matter of sheer will, Hope would have raced up the hill, but the snow was knee-deep, and it felt like they were wading through cement.

She could smell the fire now and knew it wouldn't be long before the truck blew. Ian came beside her and wrapped his arm around her, urging her on but also shielding her with his body. They were mere steps from the trees when the truck exploded. Ian covered her as they dove into a snowbank, while all around them, burning pieces of the truck showered down.

When Hope dared to lift her head and look back, she knew she would never forget the heartbreaking sight of the truck full of burning Christmas trees lighting up the sky.

Ian pulled himself up beside her, but he didn't waste time bemoaning his truck or the lost cargo. "We have to keep moving. If we can get deep enough into the woods while the truck burns, we'll be able to get away."

Hope looked up at him in disbelief. Getting away meant heading deep into the mountains in a blizzard, far from help.

*Dear Lord, have mercy.*

# FOUR

They hid within the tree line, just out of sight, and watched the truck burn. "Your truck. All your trees." Hope looked up at Ian, tears welling in her eyes at the thought of all he'd lost because of her. "I'm so sorry."

Sadness flickered across his face, but he shrugged it away. "You and Emi are safe. That's all that matters. Speaking of…" He knelt beside Emi and made a face. "Who looks like a snowman?"

Emi hid her face behind Hope's legs, but she whispered. "You do. I'm a snow girl."

"Well, snow girl, we'd better start moving before the heat from the fire turns us into puddles. Ready to explore the forest?"

Emi reached for Hope's hand and clung to it. "Is it dark in the forest? I don't like the dark."

Ian nodded. "The dark can be scary. But it can be exciting too. Like an adventure. Let's pretend we have cat eyes and can see in the dark." He leaned back and squinted at her. "Do you want to walk or ride on my shoulders?"

Emi leaned into Hope. "I want to stay with Mommy," she whispered.

"Deal. But you let me know if you get tired, okay?"

Emi nodded, and Hope's heart gave a quick stutter as

she whispered a prayer of thanks. Hiding in Ian's truck had been risky, and they were still in dire straits, but God had handed her a blessing in Ian. If anyone could get them out of this alive, it was him.

Ian stood and brushed the snow off his coat. "We should get moving."

"Is there no one we can call for rescue?" Her voice sounded desperate, but she was beyond caring. Desperate was exactly how she felt.

"When I spoke to the dispatcher, she said all the roads were shut down. I'll try again, but…" He cast a look back at the burning truck. "I want to be sure we've lost those men first. There's a campground on the other side of this mountain. I've got a compass on my phone, so we'll be able to find it even in the storm." He studied her briefly before continuing. "The terrain is rough. It's going to be challenging."

She understood that he was trying to warn her without scaring Emi. "We'll do whatever we have to."

"I've noticed that about you."

He smiled as he said it, and Hope had the sudden thought that the fire wasn't the only thing capable of melting snow. Ian had a warmth about him that…that she shouldn't be focusing on. They needed to get moving.

Ian looped their backpacks over his uninjured shoulder, and in that moment, Hope realized he had nothing of his own with him. Guilt swamped her. She'd been counting her blessings, but he had lost everything because she'd chosen to hide in his truck. He hadn't kicked them out. Instead, he'd risked his life for them and continued to do so. God bless him. There was nothing she could do about it now, but somehow, when this was over, she would find a way to make it up to him.

She grasped Emi's mittened hand a little tighter and followed Ian deeper into the woods. Within minutes, she realized he hadn't been overstating in calling this trek rough. Snow covering the ground made it difficult to judge their footing, and in many places they literally had to hold hands and form a link as they moved from tree to tree trying to keep their balance in a snowstorm that would have challenged even the most agile of cats. When Ian paused for a breather, she knew it was for her and Emi more than for him, but she was too tired to be embarrassed.

"Wait here," he murmured. "Catch your breath while I circle around. I don't think there's any chance we've been followed, but we're going to have to cross the road, so I want to be certain before we risk exposure."

The snow was coming down so hard that Ian was invisible mere moments after he left them. Panic surged through Hope. Would he find his way back to them? And what would they do, stranded alone in the forest, if he didn't?

Emi tugged at her arm. "I'm hungry."

Hope's stomach growled in agreement, and the two of them laughed quietly. "I have some granola bars in my backpack, but Ian says we're going to a camp. Can you wait a little longer?"

Emi nodded, and Hope's heart filled to bursting with love for her little girl. She was such a champ. It had been the two of them against the world ever since Keith died, and she'd never been prouder of her daughter.

As they waited alone in the cold, her thoughts returned to the question that had been plaguing her mind ever since they fled. What had happened back there? Was it really just another case of workplace violence? Was it possible that she, Steve and Emi were just numbers to add to a growing list of statistics? But if so, why had the men continued to chase her? Nothing about this made any sense.

Hope shivered. Where was Ian? She had absolutely no idea how much time had passed since he left. Time had ceased to have meaning hours ago. Minutes were measured in distance covered, not hands on a clock. She shivered again. He'd been gone long enough that her toes were freezing inside her fur-lined boots.

Emi was huddled against her, but if Hope was this cold, how could her daughter possibly be warm enough?

"I think we should do a snow dance." Hope certainly wasn't in the mood for dancing, and they had to be quiet, but she needed something that would get their blood flowing and warm them up because escaping those men meant nothing if they froze to death.

"What's a snow dance?"

"Well, it starts out like this." Hope led Emi behind a wide evergreen. She raised her arms and fluttered them as she did some impromptu ballet steps. "You pretend to be a snowflake, but then the wind howls and the snow blows in all directions." She twirled herself in a circle and waved her arms wildly while she stamped her feet and flung her head back. "Can you do that?"

Emi got very still before gently unfurling her arms as Hope had done. She danced silently among the snowflakes, and Hope was lost in the beauty of the moment. Her baby girl had always loved to dance. Hope grasped her hands and soon they were swinging and twirling, heads thrown back in pure joy, embracing the ferocity of the storm—until a cracking branch stopped them in their tracks.

What had she been thinking? Hope chastised herself. There were wild animals out here, not to mention men who maybe wanted her dead, and she was dancing with her daughter in the snow. Reacting quickly, she pulled Emi down behind a snow-covered boulder. The cracking sounds increased, accompanied by mild snorting. Hope eased up so she could see over the rock and froze.

Emi poked her head up beside her mother's. "Is that a reindeer, Mommy?"

Hope was caught between awestruck and terrified. "It's an elk. See the huge antlers?"

"It's big."

Hope couldn't argue with that.

"Will it hurt us?"

Honestly, the elk looked far more peace-loving than the gunmen who'd been on her trail. "Not if we stay quiet and don't scare him. He looks like he's trying to make a bed to wait out the storm."

"But what about Mr. Ian? How will he find us if we're hiding?"

"He has a compass." Not that it would help if they moved away from the elk. They needed to stay within sight of the spot where he'd abandoned them. Gone to make sure they were safe, Hope corrected herself. It only felt like they were abandoned in the forest at the mercy of gunmen and elk.

"He already found you."

Hope's mouth opened in a scream, but Ian's gloved hand gently covered it. "Shh, shh. I'm sorry I scared you."

The elk rustled around in its bed and turned toward them.

"Stay low," Ian murmured. "We're going to crawl in the snow until we're at least a hundred feet from him. Hope, you face forward and go first. Emi, follow your mother. I'll bring up the rear, crawling backward so I can keep an eye on him."

Hope's heart thudded in her throat. Her feet were numb, her fingers frozen, and her mind felt on the verge of surrendering to hopelessness.

Ian rested a hand on her shoulder. "It's overwhelming. But you've got this. We can make it to the cabins."

"And then what?" Hope knew she sounded petulant, so she made the effort to pull herself together. If anyone had a right to complain, it was Ian, and he was trying to reassure her. "Sorry, ignore that."

Hope slowly and silently turned away from the elk and began to crawl through the drifts of snow. Her coat snagged on branches, and her legs were dead weight, but she lowered her head and powered through.

Behind her, she could hear Ian encouraging Emi. Minutes crept by as they slowly eased away from the elk. Finally, Hope heard the words she'd longed for.

"We can stop now."

Ian knew he had to give them a few minutes to rest, but he also knew they had to push on. He'd tried calling for help again, but the answer was the same. The mountain road was shut down. Even the plows couldn't get through. They were on their own until the storm passed. Since it was showing no sign of letting up, their only hope of surviving in the wilderness was to make it to the campsite before they encountered any more predators—either animal or human.

With all his heart, Ian wished there was another solution. Their choices were severely limited by terrain that was treacherous even in summertime. Now, with the landscape covered in snow, they were risking a deadly fall with every step. And they had to do it with a child.

"Hope, it's safest if Emi lets each of us hold a hand again. We'll have the other free to help us cling to the rocks, but we can't risk her slipping."

He didn't miss the tremor caused by his words, but Hope bent over to talk to her daughter, and when she stood back up, Emi tentatively reached out her hand to his. The simple gesture punched him in the heart. Painful memories of the child he'd lost assaulted him, but he shoved them aside to focus on the task at hand.

"I promise I won't let go," he whispered as he took Emi's mittened hand in his.

They trudged along for a time before the ground suddenly began to slope downward.

Ian stopped and glanced back at Hope. "I know you're frozen and tired, but we have to take this part slowly. The ground is uneven and the drop-off is very steep. We basically have to find handholds of rock to ease our way down. I'll lead the way, but each step I'll wait until you feel secure before moving, okay?"

Her head bobbed consent, so Ian turned his attention forward. Slowly, slipping and clinging to rocky outcroppings, they made their way down the face of the mountain. The journey seemed to take forever as they struggled to keep their balance with wind gusting around them. The wind was an advantage, as it helped pin them against the rocks rather than blowing them off the side, but Ian knew that could change with a single gust.

The other advantage of this dangerous situation was it kept his focus on the task at hand rather than allowing him to think too much about the destruction left behind. He prayed the snow was heavy enough to prevent his truck from igniting a forest fire and compounding the disaster.

He'd have to replace the lost Christmas trees. The veterans' center counted on the proceeds from their holiday sale to provide much-needed help to the local vets who struggled from the effects of war.

But all of those things had to be left in God's hands. Right now, he had only one assignment—get Hope and Emi safely to the cabins so they could be rescued when the storm ended.

* * *

It felt like hours had passed by the time they finally approached a stream that bordered the camp. The running water hadn't frozen, but he found a spot that was narrow enough to cross safely.

He stopped at the edge of the water. "Emi, we're almost there, but we have to cross the water here. If Mommy says it's okay, will you let me carry you across? It would be safer that way."

Emi could barely hold her head up by that point, but she turned questioning eyes to her mother. Hope wasn't in much better shape; still, she managed to nod.

"When you're ready, lift your arms so I'll know."

Emi only hesitated a moment before lifting her arms to him. Ian bent to pick her up. The throbbing pain in his arm melted away as she snuggled into his arms and wrapped her arms around him, but it was replaced with a deep ache in his heart. Ian closed his eyes, momentarily overwhelmed by the sense of loss. His own child had died along with his wife in childbirth, but if his son had lived, he would have been nearly Emi's age. Pain threatened to drive him to his knees, and Ian knew he would be useless if he allowed his thoughts to wander back in time.

He ruthlessly shoved the memories and his regrets aside. "Be careful," he called to Hope as he plunged into the creek. "There are rocks under the surface that make it slippery. If you want to wait, I can come back for you after I get Emi across."

He shook his head in bemusement as he offered, because he already knew she would make her own way through. Hope's stubborn refusal to give in to any kind of weakness was evident in even their short acquaintance. He was grateful for that trait — it had kept her alive against all odds so far.

Once Hope had reached the creek bank safely, they pushed on, able to walk side by side now that the land was flat and they only had to wade through the snow. Emi seemed content in his arms, so Ian continued to carry her. "Please don't expect much, from this cabin," he warned Hope. "It's a summer campsite mostly for tents and RVs, but there are a few rustic cabins—emphasis on the rustic."

"If it's dry and out of the wind, you'll hear no complaints from me."

Ian doubted he'd hear complaints regardless of the cabin's condition. He hoped it would be at least somewhat of a comfort after this ordeal—a safe place to sit the storm out and wait for rescue. But he had his doubts.

They broke through the woods into the clearing. Away from the shelter of the trees, the snow had accumulated more. Ian's muscles felt like rubber, so he didn't know how Hope was still standing. "Almost there," he reassured her.

She didn't answer but tipped her head slightly, indicating she'd heard.

"Walk behind me and let me plow through the snow. You can follow in my footsteps." Hope's silence betrayed her fatigue as she fell in behind him.

When they reached the steps up to the door, Ian started to put Emi down before realizing the little girl was asleep in his arms. His breath hitched as he handed her over to Hope.

He climbed the steps and reached for the door, praying it was unlocked.

It was. Finally, something was going their way. The aged wood was warped enough that it required several hard slams of his shoulder to get the door to open. The final hard blow sent him stumbling through the doorway into the dark cabin. Hope waited by the bottom of the stairs while Ian took out his phone and used the flashlight to scan the room. It was, thankfully, clean, and there was no evidence any wildlife had taken up residence.

Ian waded his way back down the steps and lifted Emi into his arms. Hope followed him up and through the doorway. She managed to shove the door shut before collapsing on the nearest chair. Ian left his flashlight propped on the table while he gently deposited Emi on the sofa and covered her with warm blankets.

He turned and surveyed the room. "It's not home sweet home, but it will do."

Hope blinked her eyes as she struggled to stay awake.

Ian grabbed a fleece throw off the bed, crossed the room and tucked it around her. "Go ahead and rest. I'll check the cabin and see else what I can find to keep us warm..."

Ian let his words drift off. Hope was already asleep.

Wind howled around the cabin, rattling the windows and seeping through the cracks just as doubts seeped into his brain, taunting Ian with the responsibility he had assumed. He knew resting here was risky, but he had no choice. Hope had reached her physical limit and there was no other shelter in the area. Yet, despite his encouraging words to her, he wasn't confident this cabin was a refuge. If the men who'd run him off the road discovered they'd escaped the truck inferno, they would resume their hunt. And, if they knew the area, this campsite was an obvious place to start.

# FIVE

Wind-driven ice pellets stung Ian's face as he made his way around the campground. Each passing moment that revealed no sign of tracks eased the weight on his shoulders.

When he was as certain as he could possibly be, he made his way back. Standing in the shelter of the building, he tried calling the sheriff again, but the only reply was a recording that all circuits were busy. They'd have to make do here until the storm eased.

He quietly let himself in the door, and stood in the entrance brushing snow from his shoulders. It was too cold in the cabin to take off his jacket, but he pulled off his knit cap and shook it out. Hope and Emi were still sleeping soundly, so he made his way to the kitchenette. He rifled through the single cabinet and found a supply of tea bags and hot chocolate. Further digging revealed a Sterno stove that must have been left over from summer camping. Happy that he could surprise them with a warm drink when they awoke, Ian set it up and then stepped outside to fill a pot with fresh snow. He took a moment to scan the campground before heading back inside. All was calm—except for the howling wind and driving snow. Their pursuers had probably chosen to seek shelter for the night.

As he set the pot over the small flame, his thoughts retraced the events of the day. Hope claimed to have no idea who was after her. Could he believe that? Ten years in the military had honed his instincts, but they seemed to fail him regularly when women were involved. His failure with his wife was proof of that. He shook off the dark thoughts. Another woman's life depended on him now. Another child's too. He couldn't let his memories and regrets distract him from keeping them alive.

While he waited for the water to heat, he dug up some mugs and a tin of old crackers to add to Hope's protein bars. It wouldn't be a feast, but they were out of the storm and that was something to celebrate.

Ian yawned. He would have been happy to take a nap like Hope and Emi, but he refused to let down his guard no matter how safe they seemed. He sat on the floor, resting his head back against the sofa, and sent off a text to his sister. Within minutes she replied with a barrage of questions demanding more information.

Ian smiled reading through them. It was a rhetorical question in his family whether his parents had destined her for detective work by giving her the middle name Nancy. As a young boy, he'd dubbed her Nancy Drew, but rather than be annoyed as he'd secretly hoped, she'd adopted Nancy as her hero. A career as an FBI agent had been a logical choice. It was a long shot, but hopefully Nancy could help him figure this out...

Whimpers interrupted his reminiscences, and Ian rolled onto his knees so he was at the same level as Emi. The little girl was caught in a nightmare. Hardly surprising given what she had endured today. Instinctively, he reached out and gently stroked her back, murmuring soothing words. "It's okay, Emi. You're safe. No one will hurt you."

When she had finally settled back into a peaceful sleep,.

he turned around, only to find Hope wide awake and staring at him.

He moved across the room and sat on the rug beside her.
"I hope that was okay?"

She didn't speak right away. She just nodded as she studied him. "You're very good with her."

Ian heard the unspoken question behind her words. "My
sister is an FBI agent, but when she was a child, she used
to have nightmares. She read too many mysteries and was
always dreaming of bad men chasing after her." He tripped
his fingers along the fringe of the rug. "When I heard Emi's
whimpers, I didn't think. I just reacted the way I'd always
calmed Nancy. I'm sorry if I overstepped."

Hope's smile was beautiful. "You calmed my frightened
child as you did your sister. The same child whose life you
saved multiple times today. There is absolutely nothing to
apologize for."

Her soft voice was a benediction to his soul. He hadn't
always been there for Nancy, any more than he had been
for his wife, and that pain was buried deep within. It wasn't
something he wanted to share with a virtual stranger, but
he appreciated her kind words nonetheless.

Ian pulled himself up and walked over to the Sterno
stove, where the pot of water now bubbled gently. "Tea or
hot chocolate?"

The look of adoration in Hope's eyes made him laugh.
He could get used to someone looking at him like that—like
some conquering hero. He pushed the thought aside. All
he'd done was offer her a hot drink. He was nobody's hero.

Hope wasn't sure how much time had passed while she
was sipping her tea when she first noticed the flash of headlights. Across the room, Ian was instantly on alert. He cast

her an apologetic look. "I hate to wake Emi, but we have to be prepared to move out."

"They could just be some other travelers seeking shelter in a storm."

They both knew that likelihood was small.

Ian moved to stand beside the window, shifting the curtain only enough to have a side view of the area in front of their cabin.

Hope quicky gathered the few things she'd removed from her backpack. She pulled her coat closed and then managed to zip Emi into her jacket and slip on a hat and gloves without fully waking her. If there was any chance of letting her baby girl sleep, she intended to take it.

"What do you see?"

"Looks like their truck, but so far no one has gotten out, so I can't be sure. They have the headlights focused on the cabins on the far side."

Hope heard the engine gun and the sound of wheels spinning in the snow.

"And now they're swinging this way. Duck."

Ian flattened his body against the wall. Hope dropped to the floor and held motionless as the headlight beams flooded the room and swept past. The engine cut off, but somehow the silence was more frightening. Had they seen something? She held on to threads of dwindling hope that they were just travelers seeking refuge.

Ian's indrawn breath severed the last clinging strands of that hope.

"Time to go. Two men have emerged." He paused and glanced toward a sleepy Emi. "They're armed," he added quietly.

Hope's heart sank at his words. Almost immediately, car doors slammed, and she heard a harsh voice issuing commands. She uttered a prayer that the heavy drifting snow had filled their footprints. If not, their hideout would be obvious. "Should we head out the back?" she whispered, the words barely audible to Ian.

He shook his head and held up a finger that she took as a sign for silence. Tension vibrated through her body as she watched Ian observing the men. She had to trust him. And pray.

Long minutes stretched out. There was no sound from outside other than the howling of the wind, and Ian didn't move from the window. Hope trembled with anxiety, knowing their lives could very well depend on what happened in the next few minutes.

Finally, Ian backed away from the window and silently crawled toward her until he was close enough to whisper in her ear. The warmth of his breath couldn't prevent the chill his words sent through her.

"It's them. One man has gone to the far end to search those cabins. The second man started at the middle cabin and seems to be headed this way."

Hope suppressed a shiver and tried to think rationally. "So we should go out the back?"

Ian shook his head, and she could feel his hair brush her cheek.

"I have something different in mind. I want you and Emi to hide in that corner out of sight. I'm going to wait by the door and listen for his progress. When he enters the cabin, I'll get him from behind."

"But wouldn't it be better just to get away…or hide until they leave?"

"If he enters this cabin, he'll see evidence we were here and immediately alert his partner. They'll be on our trail in no time." He glanced at Emi. "And there's little doubt they'll be faster than we are. This will buy us time to make our getaway."

Hope let her eyes quickly scan the room and saw he was right. The remnants of their meal, the Sterno can and dishes, would all give away their presence.

"Once I have him restrained, we can make a run for it. The back door is close to the woods. If we go out that way while the other man is still searching, we should be able to make it back into the woods before he realizes this guy is missing. By the time he finds him, we'll have gotten a good start."

Dozens of doubts and thoughts of all the ways this could go wrong formed a knot in Hope's chest, but she knew he was right. Their choices were limited to bad and worse. She nodded her acceptance. "How much time do we have?"

"I'll check. My fingers will give you an estimate of how many minutes."

Ian swiftly crawled back to the window and eased the curtain aside. Hope slid Emi into her arms and shushed her little girl's whimper as she crouched and carried her to the corner. She cuddled Emi close as she held her breath waiting for Ian's signal.

Three fingers went up.

Terror ripped through Hope's heart. She knew Ian's plan was the best option they had, but she felt so exposed and vulnerable. How was she supposed to protect her daughter from such evil when she didn't even know why they were in danger?

The sound of boots stomping on the steps cut into her thoughts, and she froze. A hand twisted the latch, and the sound echoed loudly in the silence between her breaths.

The latch held, the door stayed closed, and moments later, Hope heard him stomp back down the steps. Relief poured through her veins in a rush of warmth. She looked to Ian, but quickly noted that rather than relaxing, he was moving into position beside the back door—the one that was supposed to be their escape route. He signaled her to stay hidden.

Hope glanced down at Emi, ready to warn her to stay silent, and her heart cracked at the fear etched on her daughter's face. Instinctively, she pulled her closer and stroked her fingertips along Emi's cheek in a comforting rhythm. "Don't worry," she whispered. "Ian has this all planned."

Emi nodded bravely, and Hope's heart constricted. She turned Emi so her face was cuddled into Hope's jacket, hoping to hide whatever was about to happen from Emi's eyes.

Outside a voice called out in the distance. Hope couldn't make out the words, but she could clearly hear the reply from right outside their back door. "No sign of them, but I'm not giving up yet."

He had barely finished shouting his reply before she heard his hand on the back door latch. Her eyes widened as she realized this one was unlatched. Had Ian done that on purpose?

Hope watched frozen as the door slowly began to open. A head appeared and he scanned the room before stepping fully inside. She saw the moment his gaze settled on the Sterno stove and pot. He quickly lifted his eyes and searched the room.

Hope's heart pounded as his gaze latched onto hers.

Behind the intruder, she could see Ian silently urging her to keep the man's attention.

"Hope?"

Hope frowned at the man's questioning tone. If he'd been chasing her all this time, how did he not recognize her?

"Who's asking?" Hope fought to keep her voice level and devoid of the fear that had her quaking in her boots.

"Are you Hope Prescott?" The man's voice rose dangerously.

"Who are you?"

He raised his weapon and pointed it at Hope. "I'm the one asking questions here, not you. Answer me."

Ian decided the time for waiting was over. He put a finger over his lips for Hope to stay silent and waited until the man began to speak.

"This is your last—"

Ian stepped forward and struck the side of the man's neck, sending him to the floor in an unconscious heap. He quickly used a dish towel as a gag and told Hope to grab the rope he had pulled from the cabinet earlier. Once he had the man completely restrained, he pulled off his belt and used it to secure him to the table. Then he ran to the window to make sure no one had heard the disturbance. By then the man was coming to, but with the gag in his mouth, there was nothing he could do to prevent their escape.

"Let's go," Ian said quietly. "There's no way he can escape. There's a truck down by the last cabin. We can use that. By the time his friend realizes what happened, we'll be long gone and the snow should cover our tracks."

Ian picked up his pack and walked to the open door. He peered out, and when the coast was clear, he beckoned to Hope and Emi. Once they were out the door, he shut it silently behind them, lifted Emi into his arms and made a run for the tree line. When they were safely out of sight, he set Emi down beside Hope. "Wait here."

He snapped off a broken pine branch and ran back, dragging the broom behind him to erase their footprints. When he reached the steps, he lifted the broom and ran toward the end cabin, leaving exaggerated prints behind. After he had passed two cabins, he lowered the branch behind him again and ran into the woods, leaving no footprints behind as he circled back to Emi and Hope.

"I'm guessing there's no truck for us to use," Hope muttered ruefully.

Ian shook his head. "Sorry. That was a ruse to buy us additional time. We're strictly on foot."

"Figured as much. But where are we going?"

"For now, just safely away from here. Once I know we haven't been followed, we can try the sheriff again or call my sister if he doesn't respond." Ian tried to put on a good face. "It's not the best solution, but…"

"It's the best available one," Hope finished for him. "Lead on."

Ian lifted Emi once again. The little girl no longer hesitated when he held her but instead burrowed against his chest. That should have made him smile, but instead it saddened him that she understood the danger too well to protest. The weight of her in his arms brought other pain to his heart, but he shoved that away.

Grasping Hope's hand, he pulled her along beside him and gestured to a coil of rope he'd tied around his waist earlier. "I looped this rope around my waist so you would have something to hold on to and a way to get my attention. I know you'd probably prefer to walk side by side, but this way I can shield you from the wind and you can walk in my footsteps. Okay?"

Like her daughter, Hope was too weary to object. She just nodded.

Ian looped the other end of the rope around her wrist and tucked it into her gloved hand. "Ready?"

She nodded again.

Ian cast a glance over his shoulder to make sure they were not being followed. He was optimistic that his strategic maneuvers would succeed in getting them safely away, because he'd noticed one important fact about his opponent—he was not dressed for hiking through the wilderness. Hopefully neither was his partner.

Ian forged his way through the heavy snow, keeping his head down and shielding Emi with his body. He wished he could do more for Hope, but he could tell that keeping her daughter safe meant more to her than her own comfort.

For an hour they kept moving forward into the swirling snow. Not once in that time did Hope tug on his rope, and his admiration for her grew with each difficult step. Finally, deciding that enough time had passed to be sure they hadn't been followed, he led them into the shelter of a cluster of trees.

One look at Hope, and Ian knew they had to stop. He took stock of their surroundings and decided they were safe enough here. "Let's stop and rest. We need to eat and drink."

Hope barely acknowledged his words, so he urged her to sit against a tree. She stumbled, nearly face-planting against the tree, but Ian grasped her just in time. He guided her until she was seated and then set Emi down beside her. He slung off the backpack and worked the frozen zipper until he got it open enough to pull out the Mylar blanket, some beef jerky and a semifrozen water bottle that he'd grabbed from the cabin.

He helped Hope to wrap the blanket around them, and then handed her the jerky. "You might break a tooth trying to bite this, so try to let it soften in your mouth. Even if you just suck on it, you'll get an energy boost."

Her lack of response was frightening. "Hope?"

She raised her head and looked at him with eyes that were glazing over. Guilt was quickly followed by fear in his gut. He'd pushed her too far. He unscrewed the cap from the water bottle and pushed it into her hand. "Drink some water."

She numbly did as he directed.

Emi huddled against her mother under the blanket, but Ian was less worried about her. He knew he'd kept her warm with his body heat, and she hadn't been exerting herself the way her mother had.

Ian watched as Hope dutifully swallowed the cold water and shivered. Drinking ice water was not wise in this environment, but it was better than dehydrating. While she sucked on the jerky, Ian pulled out his phone and tried to reach the sheriff's office once again. This time he couldn't even get a signal. They must be too far into the mountains now.

"Hope, look at me."

She lifted her head again.

"I want you and Emi to stay here. I'm going to walk out on the ridge to see if I can get a signal to call for help."

Despair filled her eyes, and in that moment, Ian would have done anything to be able to promise rescue. He squatted down in front of her. "I'll be right back."

He took a moment to note their coordinates on his phone before heading off through the trees. He was half-frozen himself, but he had to find a way to get help. Fighting a sense of failure as strong as any of these roaring winds, Ian trudged through the deep snow. He'd been pushing so hard to escape the killers, but those men weren't the only threat.

If he didn't find help or shelter, they would die out here. And it would be his fault.

# SIX

She was so sleepy.

All Hope wanted to do was snuggle under the blanket with Emi and go to sleep. Did that mean she was dying? She shivered and tried to pull Emi closer to keep them warmer, but her hands and arms didn't want to cooperate. Wasn't lack of coordination a sign of hypothermia? Her brain was working too slowly to be sure.

Where was Ian? Were they going to die out here alone in the wilderness? Would everyone think they had just disappeared? Would anyone find their bodies, or…?

Hope's mind was processing well enough to cut off the thoughts before they got too gruesome. She pulled the Mylar blanket tighter to keep out the wind that cut through them like blades of ice.

"Emi. Are you awake?" Her daughter's head moved up and down against her side. "Are you very cold?" Again Emi nodded. "I'm going to pull you onto my lap so you can be warmer against me."

Hope didn't know why she hadn't thought of that sooner. If she pulled Emi into her lap she could protect her daughter at least from the cold snow beneath them and from the wind that was the worst. At least her maternal instincts were still strong.

Snow continued to fall, and she tried to shake it off her shoulders or Ian wouldn't be able to tell them from any of the snow drifts around them.

*Ian.* Somewhere out in all this blowing white nightmare, Ian was trudging through the snow looking for help. He had to be as cold as she was, and his life was in danger because she had chosen his truck as a refuge. Her body shuddered, and this time it was guilt as much as cold that caused the tremors. If something happened to him, it would be her fault.

"Hope?"

Her heart swelled with relief at the sight of his snow-covered frame. "Over here. We're the white mountain on your right."

Ian laughed, and a pleasant warmth flooded her body at the sound.

"The silver blanket helped me distinguish you." The humor fled his voice with his next words. "I had no luck finding a signal. We're going to have to make a shelter here until the storm stops."

She must be hallucinating. This hulk-shaped being said they were camping out here. That was impossible. She started to laugh.

"Hope."

Ian crouched in front of her, concern etched on his face. It *was* him. And he *was* serious. Her laughter froze just like the rest of her. "How are you going to build a shelter out here? There's nothing but—" she looked around "—snow."

"I'm going to build us a snow cave."

Hope shuddered. "That sounds cold."

He smiled gently. "It will be better than this. But it will take me some time to build it. Are you okay for now?"

Hope nodded to reassure him, but as she did, she realized she was better. The blanket was trapping her body heat and her mind was clearing. With that clarity came concern for him. "Can I help? I've warmed up enough, I think."

"No, this is a one-person job. And honestly, I'll work more efficiently if I know you and Emi are safe."

Hope looked up at him hoping he would read the question in her eyes, the one she didn't want Emi to hear. *Are we safe?*

Ian gave a short nod. He pulled a pair of binoculars from his pack. "I borrowed these from the cabin. I searched the area as best I could through the dark and snow. I saw no sign of anyone following us, but you can keep watch if you want to help. Honestly, I think the greatest danger we face at the moment is from this storm. It shows no sign of letting up, so I need to start working on the shelter. The snow will work as a shield, but it also provides camouflage in case anyone does come looking for us. I just have to find a good-sized drift to tunnel into."

Hope studied the white landscape. "You've got plenty to choose from."

She watched anxiously as Ian got to work. Initially he seemed to wander, aimlessly poking his arm into various drifts, but once he settled on one, her anxiety transformed into amazement as she watched him tunnel his way into the huge drift. He paused periodically to check for stability and pack the snow.

Emi had fallen asleep snuggled against Hope inside the blanket, but now she stirred and stretched. She opened her eyes and looked around, clearly disoriented by the snow hitting her face. "Where are we, Mommy?"

Hope lifted an arm that was working in better coordination with her brain now and brushed the snow from Emi's cheek. "We're still in the forest, but look, Ian is building us our own snow cave."

Emi squiggled her way up, twisting until she could see, and a huge smile burst on her face. If for nothing else he had done in the past twenty-four hours, Hope's heart was near bursting with gratitude to Ian for the cave that had inspired that smile.

"What are we going to do in it?"

Hope laughed despite the desperate conditions. How could she make *We're going to wait for rescue* sound intriguing to a seven-year-old? "We're going to snuggle inside it and tell stories until our rescue team comes."

"Will we have a campfire?"

Hope scrunched her face up. "Think about that."

Emi started to giggle. "The snow would melt." She thought a little more. "Can we have a fire when we get to Christmas Village?"

Just like that, Hope's joy deflated. Explaining waiting in a snow cave was one thing. How was she supposed to explain that they were running for their lives and Christmas Village did not fit into that picture? She defaulted to the age-old line. "We'll have to wait and see." It was true, wasn't it? Maybe, if they prayed really hard, the sheriff would catch the villains who were chasing them.

Hope nearly laughed at herself then. Who was making up stories now? But the idea of people pursuing them so tirelessly preyed on her mind. She still had no idea why or what they wanted. And that man who had called her name but didn't seem to know her—who was he?

Emi squirming in her lap disrupted Hope's thoughts and she looked up to see Ian approaching them. He made a sweeping bow before them and spoke to Emi, "Your Highness, your snow castle awaits."

Emi scrambled to her feet and jumped off Hope's lap— and nearly disappeared into a snowdrift that was taller than she was. Ian scooped her up and carried her to the entrance. He set her down in the doorway he'd carved before returning to extend an arm to Hope.

She tried to push her own way up, but her legs were either still numb from the cold or had fallen asleep because as she stood, she stumbled and fell into his arms. For just a moment, she stood there, allowing him to hold her while she waited for her legs to regain their feeling. She tried to take another step, but she stumbled again.

Ian scooped her into his arms and carried her to the cave. Emi waited in the opening, clapping gleefully. "Mr. Ian carried you just like he carried me, Mommy."

Hope blushed and ducked her head. "He did because Mommy's legs went numb from someone who has been sleeping on them." She hoped the teasing words would be enough for now, because most of her mind was fighting off memories of her husband carrying her over the threshold on their honeymoon. Tears gathered in her eyes, but she angrily swiped them away. She had shed enough tears for the man who'd destroyed her dreams and ruined her life.

"If you can, it would be best to crawl inside," Ian warned. "I made the roof as stable as I could, but it's best if we don't push against it."

Happy to keep her head down, Hope crawled her way into the cave. It was small, but comfortable enough, and she was amazed at the difference it made to be out of the wind.

"How did you learn to do this?" she asked as Ian followed Emi into the center.

"I had Army training, but I also belong to a veterans' group. We go hiking in the wilderness in all seasons, so we've trained in survival techniques."

As he was talking, Ian took the Mylar blanket he'd brought in with them and spread it on the snow against the back wall.

Once he had it flat, he looked up and grinned. "That and all the years of building snow forts with my brother and sister." He gestured to the floor. "It would be best if you sat on that. I have another one you can pull around you."

Hope studied this man who was a seemingly endless font of surprises. "What about you?"

He shrugged. "I'll be fine. Make yourselves comfortable. I'm going to go take another look around outside."

After assuring himself that there was still no indication they'd been followed, Ian crawled back into the cave and immediately busied himself digging food he'd taken from the cabin out of the backpack. He'd left a note for the owners that he would replace it as soon as possible. The cave would keep them warm, but they had to be sparing in the food they ate. If they ran out of water, he could start a fire and melt snow, but he had no way of replacing their food supply.

He handed Hope a protein bar, but she immediately broke off half and handed it back to him.

"Eat. You need energy as much as we do. More, because you're doing all the work."

"I'm trained to go days without food if necessary."

She kept her hand extended. "Please. I can't eat if you won't."

Understanding that he wasn't the only one with a sense of pride and duty, Ian accepted the bar. From what he could tell of Hope, he knew that she was someone used to standing up for herself. What was her story? Where was Emi's father? None of it was his business, and yet he wondered.

"I don't suppose in any of this vaunted training, they've taught you how to predict how long a storm like this might last?"

Hope grinned as she spoke, and Ian appreciated her attempt to lighten the tension.

"Nope, but the last weather report I saw said the storm should move on by morning."

Morning seemed a long way off when you were running low on food and stranded in the wilderness. Ian checked again for a signal. He couldn't call the sheriff, but he could try to get another text through to his sister. Sometimes that worked when there wasn't enough of a signal to call.

Had to evacuate cabin. Made a snow cave. Need rescue ASAP.

He added in their coordinates and hit Send.

"God willing, my sister will get the message and arrange our rescue. Now, what shall we do to entertain Miss Emi?"

"Mommy said we can tell stories like if this was a real campout."

Hope laughed and shook her head in wonder. "What do you know about real campouts?"

"They have them all the time in my books."

A shadow crossed Hope's face at her daughter's words, and Ian wondered what she was thinking about. Was she remembering the scene back at her office? They needed to talk about that more. What had seemed like possibly an unfortunate incident of workplace violence took on a new light when you considered how relentless these men had been in their pursuit. If he wanted to talk to Hope, he needed to distract Emi. Unfortunately, the backpack didn't seem to contain anything that would interest a seven-year-old girl. What would entertain a child of that age? He had absolutely no experience to draw on.

Ian shrugged away the desolate thoughts that tried to

intrude. He gazed around the small cave, and inspiration struck. "Emi, I'm guessing you like to read, right?"

Her face lit up and he knew the answer. She nodded. "Mommy calls me a bookworm."

"I wish we had a book for you to read here, but I was thinking of something else you might like to do."

She cocked her head and waited.

"Do you know what people did before they had books?"

Emi bobbed her head eagerly. "We learned about that at school. They played telephone."

Ian looked to Hope for explanation, but she just shrugged.

"Can you explain, sweetie?" she asked.

"In the olden days they told stories, but when they told them over and over they changed. Just like when you play telephone and you tell someone a story and they tell the next person, but by the time it gets to the last person it's so different that you all laugh."

Ian did laugh and smiled at Hope. "I think your daughter just summed up prehistory."

"Are we going to play telephone?"

Her innocent question had Ian thinking of whispering in Hope's ears, and he felt a flush rise in his cheeks. He had to clear his throat before he could answer. "No, that wasn't what I was thinking. Since you read so much, I'm sure you know about the cavemen, right?"

"Oh, yes."

Ian was tempted to ask for her take on them, but he reminded himself he was creating a distraction because he needed to talk to Hope. "Have you heard about how they told stories by drawing pictures on the walls of their caves?"

Her face lit up with interest, and Ian vowed to show her drawings from the Chauvet and Lascaux caves once they were safe. For now, he'd have to inspire her imagination.

"The cavemen used sticks and different kinds of dyes to tell stories by drawing pictures on the cave walls. They did such a great job of it that their drawings lasted for thousands of years and people go on trips into the caves to see them."

"Can we go there, Mommy?"

Hope smiled and hugged her daughter. "Maybe. But not tonight."

Emi looked back at Ian. "So, what are we going to do?"

"I thought you might like to make drawings on our cave walls. We don't have colored dyes, but you could use my pencil and carve them into the ice."

"What would I draw?"

"That's up to you. You think of a story." Ian was making this up as he went, but he seemed to have hit on something that engaged Emi, so he ran with it. "Want me to do one first?"

She bobbed her head. "Yes, please."

Ian thought hard for a moment, and then picked up the pencil he'd dug out of his pack. He walked over to the wall closest to the door and began to sketch a stick figure on the snow. Emi hung back at first, but with Hope's prompting, she came over to watch. He'd noticed that about her. She had a natural reserve that only lifted when she was safely within arm's reach of Hope. Was she just shy? Or had something in her young life given her cause to be cautious?

Ian glanced at Emi and added a hat and pigtails just like she had. Then he started to sketch his dog. He wasn't much of an artist, but few kids could reject a dog.

"Is that me?" Emi asked softly, and he didn't miss the note of longing in her voice. He smiled down at her. "It is, and this is Rocco. He was my dog when I was your age."

"That's a funny name for a dog."

"He was a funny dog." He held out the pencil to her.

"Do you want to make up stories about the adventures of Emi and Rocco?"

She glanced at Hope, who nodded. "Okay. Thank you, Mr. Ian."

Once Emi was lost in her world of drawings, Ian crossed the cave to sit beside Hope.

"Thank you for entertaining her."

"You're welcome. But I confess I had an ulterior motive. We need to talk."

"About what happened?"

He tilted his head toward hers so he could whisper his thoughts. "Yes. We need to rethink the attack back at your office. Random workplace shooters don't generally follow the employees deep into a blizzard and continue their pursuit through the night."

Hope nodded. "I know. I've been thinking about that."

"Did you come up with any new ideas?"

"Not really. I've been rethinking those moments before Steve left my office and headed down the hallway. I told you he'd come to give us her present, tickets to Christmas Village, but I had this nagging sense something was wrong. I asked him about it, but he said we'd talk after Christmas."

"That's something. I don't want to make you relive it, but I think we have to reexamine every part of it. You never know what else you might remember." He paused to allow Hope to gather her composure. "When you got the alert, what did you do?"

"I ran to close the door, but…" She hesitated. "I couldn't resist looking. I wanted to help Steve. I couldn't just abandon him."

"Did you see anything?"

"No, the hallway was still empty, but I heard shouts and gunfire."

She closed her eyes, so Ian waited in silence. It appeared she was trying to replay the scene and he didn't want to interrupt any part of it.

She finally opened her eyes and looked up at him. "I didn't see anyone, so I slammed the door and followed our procedure to evacuate." She gave an involuntary shudder. "But I know they were definitely after me. As Emi and I were escaping to the parking lot, we heard them talking. They said that Steve told them I'd left." She choked on a sob. "Then one told the other that maybe if they hadn't hurt him, Steve, they could've found out more about where I was or where I might have gone."

Ian tried to stay calm, although every nerve in his body was thrumming with anger. "There was nothing they said or nothing unique about their voices that could give them away?"

Hope shrugged. "Not that I noticed."

Ian ground his teeth in frustration. "It makes no sense, unless... You don't have any enemies, do you?"

Hope smiled briefly. "Not that I know of. I mean, my life is pretty simple. Work, Emi's school, food shopping. Not very exciting."

Ian wanted to ask about Emi's father, but he couldn't find a tactful way to bring him up. "I hate to say this because I don't want to scare you, but I think it's safe to assume they won't give up."

Beside him, Hope's entire body wilted. "I know. I pretty much figured the same. But what do I do to avoid them if I don't know who they are or what they want?"

Ian was about to answer, to try to give some vague assurance, when his phone buzzed. He glanced down at the message. "It's from my sister." He frowned as he read. "She says the front stalled over us, and the snow is still falling at a fast rate even down in the valley. She'll come to rescue us as soon as she can get through."

Hope made a valiant attempt at a smile. "At least if she can't get through yet, we can hope the bad guys can't either."

Ian didn't want to dash her fragile hopes, but the bad guys weren't his only concern. The cave had them warm enough that they wouldn't freeze to death, but they were running out of food. Even if he held back on eating, it was just a matter of time before there was nothing left.

# SEVEN

"Emi's not the only one who loves stories," Hope murmured as she and Ian sat alone in the darkness. Emi had finally tired of drawing and had snuggled up asleep in the blanket beside her mother. Hope was cold and hungry, and in need of distraction. Getting to know her handsome rescuer seemed like a good idea.

"You want to make cave drawings?"

Hope laughed. "No, I want to learn about you. Tell me about your life out here. What it's like to run a Christmas tree farm."

Ian was quiet for a moment. "It's a lot of hard work, but I like the physicality of it. After the war, I needed to find a purpose, a way of keeping my mind and body busy. Working a long day makes it easier to sleep at night."

Hope sensed some brutal truth underlying that answer, but she didn't push. She knew of the toll war had taken on veterans, and she remembered Ian's voice when he'd spoken of delivering trees for the fundraiser. "I'm sorry my trouble made you lose your trees. I hope you'll let me pay to replace them."

"Not necessary. There are plenty more back at the ranch where those came from, and I seriously doubt anyone is out Christmas tree shopping in this weather. Think no more of it."

*And don't ask any more questions about it either.* That was the message Hope took away, so she changed the topic.

"Do you have children? Back at the ranch, I mean."

"Why do you ask?" His voice was dry, and he had to clear his throat to get the words out.

A sense of unease left Hope unsure how to answer. She hadn't meant any harm by asking, but there was a quality to his response that made her realize this was an uncomfortable topic as well.

"I'm sorry. You're so good with Emi. It seems natural. I just thought..." Her voice trailed off.

"She's a scared child."

"Yes, and you kept her physically safe," Hope replied, feeling on safer ground. "But it was more than that. You respected her feelings. I think she recognized that and it made her feel emotionally safe too."

Ian cleared his throat again. "We're trained in how to treat children."

She accepted his brusque explanation, sure once again that she was treading on sensitive personal space. She owed him the same respect for his feelings that he'd shown Emi.

"Well, thank you."

Ian's voice was hoarse. "No problem."

She felt him shift and stand before he spoke again. "I'm going to go stand watch."

"Please don't." Hope stood, too, and reached for his arm. She missed in the dark and stumbled forward. Ian's arms came up to catch her, and she felt the tension in his body. She held very still. "I'm sorry. I shouldn't have pried."

They stood in silence, inches apart, something new and raw filling the air between them. "I was married once. My wife and child died in childbirth."

He turned and headed out of the cave, leaving Hope's heart breaking for the pain she'd heard in his voice.

* * *

Ian crawled back out of the cave entrance to give himself a bit of breathing room. He gratefully accepted the slap of frigid air. Hope's innocent question had touched a little too close for comfort. He regretted brushing her off, but he wasn't about to divulge his heartbreak to a woman he'd known for less than a day, no matter how intense the experience had been. There was something about life-and-death struggles that bonded you quickly, but that didn't entitle her to his entire sad story.

It was only Hope's vulnerability that was tugging at his heart, he assured himself. There was something so vulnerable about this duo that he couldn't quite put his finger on, but he suspected it went deeper than what had happened yesterday.

When he'd taken them into his truck, he'd assumed responsibility for their safety. He would do whatever it took to get them to the sheriff. Then he would go back to his ranch, pick up a new load of trees to replace the ones damaged in the fire and go on about his life—however lonely it might seem.

And it was going to be lonely. He could be honest with himself about that much. In less than twenty-four hours, Hope and Emi had winnowed their way into his life and his heart, resurrecting the thoughts he usually kept deeply hidden, reminding him of all he'd lost.

Ian stood and walked out into the cold. With the wind howling in his face, he breathed in deeply and closed his eyes against the onslaught of ice and snow. The pain felt right, normal. Together with regret and a swamping sense of guilt, it defined his days. He needed that pain now to remind himself that sweet Emi and her mother weren't just a reminder of all he had lost. They offered a glimpse of a life he no longer deserved.

# EIGHT

Hope woke to the sound of jingling bells and her daughter's excited voice.

"It's nine days 'til Christmas, Mommy." Emi squirmed against her. "Remember? Today we find a Christmas tree." She shoved her device in front of Hope's face. "But the app's not working."

Hope rubbed her eyes and looked from Emi's blank screen to the rounded white walls, waiting for something to make sense in her foggy brain.

At least she understood the problem with Emi's device. "We don't have internet out here."

She'd been working on marketing the platform for Twelve Days 'til Christmas for the better part of the last year, and the success of it had driven Steve's company's profits into the stratosphere.

*Steve.* Her heart sank as memories of the past day came rushing at her. The invasion, being run off the road—several times—escaping the camp and trudging through endless miles of wilderness until finally ending up here. She and Emi were in a cave made of snow in the middle of a forest in the dead of winter. And somehow, they hadn't frozen to death. That was thanks to Ian. But what had happened to Steve?

She opened her phone hoping for news, but there was still no service.

And where was Ian?

After her rude intrusion into his life story last night, he'd gone outside to stand watch. Of course, he hadn't said that was the reason, but she'd seen something shift in his eyes when she asked about children. On top of all the danger she'd brought into his life, now it seemed she'd also caused him pain. And that was the last thing she wanted to do.

He must have come back in once she and Emi were asleep because the other blanket had been used. She had a strong sense that while he might have used it to keep warm, he likely hadn't slept a wink. She was already getting to know he had an overdeveloped protective instinct, for which she was extremely grateful.

"Mommy, do you hear those bells?"

Hope pushed her thoughts aside and listened while she dug out the last piece of protein bar and handed it to her daughter. "I do hear the bells. Ian said his sister was going to come with horses, so maybe she's here." Was it possible they were finally going to be rescued?

Hope pushed her hair out of her face and finger-combed the long blond tresses. She hated to even think what she must look like, but she had no way of fixing her appearance. Giving up, she reached for the last water bottle and handed it to Emi. She sure hoped that the bells meant horses, because they were down to the last bottle of water and were out of food.

The sound could mean danger too, of course, but Hope felt no fear. Logically, someone coming to cause them harm was unlikely to herald their arrival with jingling bells. She knew, though, that her feeling of security was due more to Ian's protection than logic. Still, she held Emi back from running out to see if there were truly horses until Ian poked his head in the cave entrance and called out for her.

"Emi, are you awake? I think you're going to want to see this."

Emi tugged at her hand. "Come, Mommy. Let's go."

Hope fell to her knees and crawled after her daughter. Emi's squeal of delight made her crawl faster. When she emerged, weak sunlight was filtering through snow that still drifted lightly to the ground, but her attention was drawn immediately to Emi, who stood in shock, hands cupped over her mouth.

Hope turned to follow the direction of Emi's gaze, and her own mouth fell open in surprise. Reindeer? Was she imagining things? She looked over at Ian, who was watching Emi's reaction with pure delight. When he finally looked her way, she just slowly shook her head and smiled. "Thank you."

Hope and Emi watched in awe as the reindeer pulled a sleigh over the snow-covered slope. "I thought you said she was bringing horses."

"I did, but I guess the drifts were too much for the horses. Reindeer have webbed feet that let them walk on top of the snow."

"Like ducks."

Ian laughed. "Very big ducks, Emi. You already know I grow Christmas trees on our ranch, but my sister raises reindeer too. They're her special project."

"Your sister the FBI agent?"

Ian smirked. "I spend a lot of time filling in for her on reindeer duty. But she loves them like they're her children."

There was that word again. *Children*. But Ian said it without flinching this time, so Hope let it go.

"This is amazing. I've never seen a reindeer outside of a movie."

The sleigh pulled up beside them, and a woman jumped

down to greet them. She threw her arms around Ian and hugged him tight. "You had us worried, bud."

"Emi, Hope, this is my baby sister, Ellen, otherwise known as Nancy Drew."

Nancy rolled her eyes. "Did he tell you that story?"

Ian shrugged. "No, just that you loved reading mysteries."

Hope watched the interplay between brother and sister, and a tightness banded her chest. She was an only child, and since her husband had died, Emi would be too. Hearing Ian talk about his family had warmed her heart, and now seeing their evident bond reminded her of the hopes she'd once had to build a big family of her own.

"Hope?"

She shook herself. This was neither the time nor the place for dark memories. "Yes?"

"I was just saying we should get going right away. Nance says there is no good news about the incident at your office, which means…" He glanced toward Emi. Her daughter was totally entranced by the reindeer and probably wouldn't hear his words, but she appreciated his tact. She didn't need him to finish the sentence. The attackers were still on the loose.

"I just have to grab my pack."

"I'll get it. I want to grab the blankets too. Why don't you bring Emi over to meet the reindeer with Nancy while I get our stuff?"

"You really call her that?"

He laughed. "It started out as a joke, but it became her nickname. She never really liked her real name after that. I think Emi will like her. She's a bookworm too—when she's not catching bad guys or caring for reindeer."

Emi stood by Nancy's side, which told Hope exactly how excited she was by the animals. Normally with strangers she hid behind Hope, but something about Ian and his sister seemed to cut through her reserve.

Nancy waved her over as Ian headed back into the cave.

"Thank you so much for coming out in the storm…" Hope smiled. "I don't know what to call you," she admitted. "It doesn't seem right to use a family nickname."

Nancy grinned back. "These days the only people who call me Ellen are my bosses. Even my coworkers call me Nancy. Not sure I'd remember to answer if you called me anything else."

Nancy guided them toward the reindeer, but Hope and Emi stayed a healthy distance back as she approached them and stroked the big head. "Hope, Emi, I'd like you to meet my best friends."

"What are their names?" Emi asked softly.

"This is Sundancer. And over here is Conner. Splasher and Glitzen stayed back at the ranch."

Emi grinned. "Those sound almost like—"

"Shh," Nancy teased. "They already think they're too cool pulling my sleigh. Let's not give them any ideas."

Emi giggled and Hope's heart danced. Maybe Emi would remember this as a grand adventure involving reindeer rather than being traumatized by the experience.

She couldn't ignore the fact that they were still in danger, though, and Nancy had clearly not forgotten either. Hope noticed how the FBI agent's gaze was constantly roaming the hillside even as she chatted with them. She was on full alert, which meant Hope needed to be too.

"Should I get Emi settled so we can move out?"

Nancy nodded solemnly. "I don't like the isolation out here now that the storm has petered out."

She showed Hope how to climb into the sleigh and then

lifted Emi up. "You two take the back seat. Ian and I will ride up front to keep watch."

She strode across the snow to meet Ian and help him with the bags.

"You didn't say she was cute."

The words drifted on the air, catching Hope's ear.

"Emi? She's seven and adorable," Ian replied.

Nancy punched his arm. "Yeah, she is, but I meant the mother."

Hope couldn't help but stare, wanting to see his reaction. He tilted his head and looked down. "Let's not go there, okay?"

There was nothing teasing in that reply, and Hope's heart gave a little lurch. Ian had a story, and she knew his hadn't had any happier an ending than hers.

Nancy dumped the two backpacks in the back seat and handed the blankets to Hope while Ian circled the sleigh and climbed in the other side. She picked up the reins and flicked them gently. As the reindeer took off, flying across the snow, with Emi squealing in glee, Nancy pointed to the bag beneath Ian's seat. "Mom sent some thermoses full of coffee and hot cocoa. I think there are some doughnuts in there too. She thought you might be hungry."

Ian glanced back at Hope who nodded. He poured a steaming mugful of cocoa and carefully passed it back to her. "This one's for Emi, but it's hot, so be careful."

Hope took the mug and held it so Emi could blow on it. The cocoa cooled quickly in the freezing air, so she snuggled her daughter into the blanket and handed her the mug. When Ian passed her a napkin holding fresh-baked cinnamon doughnuts, she inhaled and murmured, "I think I already love your mother."

Ian handed her a mug of coffee. "This should cinch it. My mother makes the best coffee ever."

Hope thought hot anything would have been a blessing, but when she sipped the hot, sweet coffee, she closed her eyes in bliss.

She settled back into the blanket beside Emi and slowly sipped her coffee while the reindeer pranced through the snow. She'd lost all sense of time and place while fleeing in the storm, but now the wind had eased, and scraps of blue sky peeked between the clouds as the storm blew eastward. She sighed. There was still danger, and so many questions needing answers, but for the moment she was content to count her blessings—Ian and his family being at the top of the list.

That sense of peace didn't last long. The sound of engines caught her ear first, and then she noticed how rigidly Ian and Nancy were sitting. They were both scanning the forested mountainside and were on full alert. Hope saw Nancy gesture toward the floor, and Ian bent and picked up a rifle. That was when Hope noticed Nancy already had one resting on her lap.

"What should we do?" she asked quietly.

Ian deferred to Nancy, who spoke urgently. "Get down on the floor. Hide the Mylar blankets under you because the silver will make you a target. There are lap rugs on the floor. Pull them over you. Better to get you hidden before they see you."

Her no-nonsense instructions sent adrenaline rushing through Hope's body. Her limbs went tingly, and she felt the same lack of coordination the cold had caused. Pulling herself together, she took the empty cocoa cup from Emi and helped the little girl settle in the well behind the front seat. Hope climbed down beside her and pulled the blankets over them like an awning. And then she began to pray.

\* \* \*

Ian glanced at his sister. Truth be told, there was no one he'd rather have beside him in this moment than Nancy. Her instincts were excellent and her marksmanship was even better. He hoped their combined skills were enough because they were open targets out here in the middle of nowhere.

The sound of the snowmobiles got louder.

"Could just be people out for fun after the storm," he suggested.

"Could be."

Her clipped tone matched his doubts.

"There. See that flash on the south mountain?" Nancy murmured. "The sun just glanced off a rifle barrel."

Ian trained his eyes in the direction she'd indicated. He could make out two snowmobiles. The lead one had a rifle aimed in their direction. "Do you think they're in range yet?" He was trained military, but his sister knew these mountains, and he trusted her judgment.

"Close, but they're still moving, so it will be hard to hit the target from there."

The target. *Them.*

"How do you want to handle it?" Ian asked.

"If we were on flatter ground, I'd give the boys their head and let them run for it. Pretty sure they can't outrun a snowmobile, but they're fast."

Ian would have smiled were the situation not so serious. Nancy's pride in her reindeer was legendary in their family. "But we're not on flat ground. So?"

"Your call. How much of a risk do you feel like taking?"

Ian didn't have to think long. The lives of the precious child and her mother hiding behind their seat were not something he was willing to risk. "None."

Nancy flashed him a glance, and Ian knew he would

have some explaining to do later. He was not known for his cautious nature, but he was not willing to risk the life of an innocent child.

"Then we make for rough ground," Nancy decided. "It will be tough on the humans and the sled, but my boys can handle rocky slopes better than a snowmobile can. The snow should cushion the worst of it."

"Hope?"

"Do whatever you have to. We'll manage."

Nancy nodded her approval. "I'll try to narrate what we're doing so you aren't surprised. My plan is to get down this rocky slope and head across the stream. If they know what they're doing, they'll skip the snowmobiles across, but once we're on the other side, I can let the boys have their heads."

"Emi, do you know how fast reindeer can run?" Ian asked.

"No," came a tremulous voice from beneath the blanket. "Can't they fly?"

Nancy choked on a laugh. "That would sure be a help if they could. My reindeer aren't the kind that can fly. But they run very fast. It will almost feel like flying."

Ian appreciated his sister's steady humor, but the fact was, reindeer couldn't outrun a snowmobile. Any advantage they had from their surefootedness was lost because they were carting the sleigh. No two ways about it—they were in trouble again.

Since Nancy had to keep a close eye on the terrain ahead, Ian turned in his seat to watch their pursuers. A rifle shot exploded in the air as the reindeer raced across the snow, eliminating any question about intent. Fortunately, the shot went wide and drove harmlessly into the snow a safe distance back.

"We okay?" Nancy whispered.

"So far. The lead driver is gaining, but his aim is off so far. I'm going to take a shot to warn them back. Hope, keep Emi down. I'm going to be shooting over your head." Ian locked the rifle into position and aimed. He counted down quietly so Nancy would know when to expect the shot. "Three, two, one."

He fired at the lead snowmobile. The driver zigzagged. Ian hadn't expected to hit them, since they were still too far out of range, but perhaps they'd be less aggressive if they knew they would draw return fire.

"Hold on," Nancy warned him as she called to Hope. "Rocky ride approaching."

Ian swiveled to look forward just in time to see Nancy swerve the reindeer into a stand of pine trees. The distance between the trees was barely wider than the sleigh, making the task somewhat like threading a needle, but Nancy's hands stayed steady on the reins, and she barely flinched as the branches brushed the sides of the sleigh. "Nice work."

Nancy only huffed out a breath in reply as she continued to thread her way between the trees. "Good thing I didn't bring the big sleigh."

"This was a good move. I can get a better aim at them now because they can't zigzag in the trees." Ian turned to kneel on the floor of the sleigh and level the rifle across the seat back.

He waited until both snowmobiles had entered the trees before firing again. This time his bullet bounced off the windshield, and the driver momentarily lost control.

"Good news, bad news. I hit him. But that means they're in range. Can you slump down below the seat and still drive the sleigh?"

"Enough to make me less of a target. You?"

"I'll sit to the side and only pop up to shoot."

Ian eased up so he could see, and a bullet whizzed by his head. This wasn't looking good. The narrow confines helped the enemy as well as them because the trees helped frame the shot better than a wide-open field of snow. "How much longer in the forest?"

"About a hundred feet," Nancy answered. "Then we exit into a stream. That should at least give them a moment's pause."

Another shot hit the rear runner, and the force of it vibrated through the sleigh. Ian heard a muffled cry from the back seat, and his heart ached. No child should have to endure this. That had been one of the hardest parts of being a soldier for him—seeing the impact of war on children. He was not going to let these men get Emi if it was the last thing he did.

It wouldn't be smart to raise his head again, so Ian leaned over the side of the sleigh and took two quick shots. A cry told him at least one shot had hit its mark.

"Good job," Nancy praised. "Now hold your fire. We're going into the water."

Ian crouched down in the seat and grabbed hold of the side rail as he braced himself. The reindeer dashed right into the running water, but the sleigh jolted as it hit the rocks. A layer of snow had built up on them, but the fiercely flowing water kept it from accumulating enough to make an easy ride. He wondered how the snowmobilers would handle the transition from ground to water.

"I don't understand how they found us," he said quietly to Nancy.

She was concentrating on pulling the sleigh out of the stream and onto a stretch of deep open snow. "I don't think they followed me," she replied as she gave the reindeer their heads to race across the shimmering snow. "They approached from the opposite direction. Most likely they waited for the snow to end, grabbed some snowmobiles and headed out in the direction you'd gone. Did you track straight or weave?"

Ian muttered under his breath as he took another shot. "I tried to follow my compass, but we couldn't see a thing in the wind and driving snow, so mainly I just kept going. I knew they weren't dressed for the weather, so I figured they couldn't follow us too far."

Nancy chuckled as she carefully glanced over her shoulder. "I guess that explains their current predicament."

Ian looked back and laughed in a combination of relief and amusement. "First rule of snowmobiling. Don't stop in soft powder." As he watched, the snowmobiles were slowly sinking into the snow as the men stood and pointed their rifles.

"Heads down."

Rifle fire cracked through the air as Nancy urged the reindeer ahead. "Gee-haw."

The air around them exploded with repeated shots that fell short as they drew out of range.

Ian released a sigh of relief once they were safely away. Nancy slowed the sleigh so Hope and Emi could climb out of the well and settle back onto the seat. "Everybody okay?"

Ian watched Hope nod, but he could see how badly her body was trembling. "It'll be okay now. We'll be at the ranch soon."

Nancy gave him a sidelong glance, and Ian shrugged. They both knew he was offering a false promise. These men had proved one thing very clearly. They didn't give up easily, and they'd be back on their trail before long. The question remained—why?

# NINE

"Those are our parents standing on the porch waving at you," Ian chuckled as the sleigh pulled up to a beautiful log-cabin-style ranch house. White lights twinkled along the roofline and green garlands were draped across the porch. Best of all, smoke curled from a chimney. For the first time, Hope felt her lips curve in a genuine smile.

The house represented a home and warmth, good people, family…and peace.

And she was bringing danger to their doorstep.

Hope leaned forward to speak to Ian. "I can't stay here."

"Of course you can. My parents will be thrilled to meet you and Emi. Nancy told them we were coming."

Hope shook her head vehemently. "I can't risk their lives. You know what these men are like, what they'll do to get to me. I just need a ride to the sheriff."

Ian frowned and looked at Nancy. "You tell her."

Nancy pulled back on the reins and the sleigh came to a rest. "There's no use arguing with my mother. But it's okay. Both Ian and my father are former military. I'm with the FBI. My other brother isn't here because he's deployed, but you don't need to worry. We've got you covered."

Hope sputtered in frustration. "I wasn't questioning your ability. It's just, I've already asked too much of you. I don't want to drag the rest of your family into a mess I don't even understand. I don't want to cause any more trouble."

Nancy laughed. "You don't know our mother. She will not take no for an answer."

Hope was out of time to convince them because Ian's mother was already hustling down the steps, welcoming words on her lips.

"Told you," Nancy teased. "Don't mind her," she added, glancing at Emi. "She's just dying for some grandbabies of her own."

Hope felt Ian stiffen. Was it the baby mention or Nancy's not-so-subtle implication?

"I heard that, Nancy." Mrs. Fraser wagged her finger playfully. "You just shush. This little lamb has had a terrible fright," she continued as Ian helped Hope and Emi down from the sleigh. She crouched beside Emi. "We need to get you all warmed up. How does a bubble bath sound?"

Emi looked to Hope, who could only shrug. She knew how to accept when she'd lost a battle. At least temporarily. "Honestly anything with hot water sounds good to me right now. Thank you, Mrs. Fraser."

"Oh dear, no. We're not so formal here. You just call me Sarah. Now come on in. Poppa has a fire burning in the hearth, so once you get washed up, we can settle in and have lunch by the fireplace."

Hope mustered a smile that she hoped was warmer than she felt. "Thank you, Sarah. You're too kind. I don't…"

But Ian's mother was already hustling Emi into the warmth of the house. She shrugged and turned to grab their backpacks before following. From the other side of the sleigh, she could hear Nancy's voice.

"She sure is different from Shelby."

Hope had no idea who Shelby was, but the comment

clearly upset Ian. She couldn't hear his reply, but the look on Nancy's face told her it was not all in fun.

Feeling guilty for overhearing something that was clearly not meant for her, Hope grabbed the packs and hurried up the front steps. She caught up just in time to see Emi's re-action as she stepped into the house. Her daughter was speechless with wonder, and Hope had to admit, it was a pretty amazing sight. They'd walked into a Christmas wonderland.

A huge tree decorated in white lights and handmade or-naments dominated one side of the large room. Fairy lights twinkled in evergreen boughs that hung from the rafters. Soft Christmas music played in the background and the scent of pine filled the air, mixing with the aroma of bak-ing, but it was the roaring fire in the stone fireplace on the opposite wall that beckoned Hope.

"It's like Christmas Village but inside," Emi whispered in awe as she spun in a slow circle trying to take it all in. Hope felt a bit like a kid herself. Everywhere she looked there was something else to notice, but the effect wasn't overwhelming at all. It was welcoming and felt like what she thought coming home at Christmas should feel like— warm and inviting. Unexpected tears pricked her eyes, and she quickly blinked them back.

This wonderful room only reinforced her conviction that they couldn't stay here. They couldn't bring danger to this family or home. She would clean up and let Emi recover and eat, but then Ian would have to take her to the sheriff or she'd call him to come get her.

An hour later, warm from the bath and cozy in some fleece-lined clothing Sarah had brought her, Hope was struggling to maintain her resolve. Everyone in Ian's fam-ily was just so nice, so welcoming. When she entered the kitchen, she had to stop and smile. Her normally shy daughter was chattering away as she stood on a step stool helping Ian's mother arrange cornbread on a platter for lunch. What was it about this family that brought out the best in her daughter?

Another burst of longing hit Hope, and she quickly ducked her head. The acceptance and love in this room represented everything she had ever wanted. Everything she thought she'd have when she married Keith. Everything that had proved to be nothing but an illusion built on her pipe dreams and starry eyes.

Was that what she was doing now? Imagining what she wanted to find?

"Hope, you're just in time to help bring the food to the table."

And just like that, her negative thoughts evaporated as she was caught up in the happy bustle of a loving family.

When everyone was gathered around the table near the hearth, they joined hands and bowed their heads as Ian's father led them in a prayer of thanksgiving for the meal they were blessed to share. After a rousing chorus of amens, the food was passed and happy chatter resumed. Hope found herself feeling like she was caught in some twilight zone. Outside lay danger, men she didn't know shooting at her and pursuing her with a determination that defied her understanding.

But in here, the spirit of Christmas reigned with peace, love and joy, laughter and good conversation. She leaned down to offer Emi another helping of cornbread and beef stew and was shocked out of her happy mood at the sight of her child's sad face.

"What's wrong, love?" she whispered as she slid her arm around her daughter's narrow shoulders.

Emi sniffled, and Hope's heart squeezed, fearing the days of terror had caught up with her. "You can tell me."

Emi looked up, eyes shining pools of unshed tears. "We missed two days of the countdown. We'll never win now."

Hope bit back a smile. This she could deal with. "You know the point of Twelve Days 'til Christmas was never about winning. That's the number-one rule. It's all about the fun."

"I know, but I *was* having fun. *And* I was winning stickers."

Hope couldn't help but smile then. Adding Christmas stickers had been one of her contributions. If she'd learned anything as a mother, it was don't come between a girl and her stickers.

"What is Twelve Days 'til Christmas?"

Hope looked up and was startled to see everyone at the table focused on them. Ian's mother had asked the question, so Hope directed her answer to her. "It's the social media platform my company created. You can play it on an app or on any computer or device. Basically, it's a countdown to Christmas with different activities to do each day. We created a safe online space that gives people a small-town community feeling. Just like towns have a calendar of events, we focus on different activities each day. The kick-off was the Christmas tree lighting on our town green—all virtual of course, but people got to share photos and videos of their families counting down and singing along."

Suddenly self-conscious with how she'd gotten carried away, Hope smiled bashfully. "I'm just a little over-the-top enthusiastic about it." She shrugged. "It's been pretty successful."

"So, Miss Emi, what were the days you missed?" Poppa asked.

Emi's pout lifted a bit as she replied. "I missed the snowball fight and we don't have a tree."

"But Emi, you got to sleep in a snow cave and do cave drawings," Ian suggested. "Doesn't that count?"

"Only if we'd had a snowball fight."

"Now she tells me," Ian teased.

"You could play with reindeer," Nancy offered. "Would that help?"

Emi brightened. "That could count for reindeer-games day, right, Mommy? But that's not for five more days." Her face fell again.

The idea that they could still be on the run from these dangerous men in five more days sucked away Hope's Christmas spirit, but she rallied for Emi's sake. "Strictly speaking, the activity doesn't have to be on the exact day. But you could use them for sleigh-rides day if you want. You did go on a sleigh ride with them."

Emi grinned at Nancy. "I bet no one else had reindeer for their sleigh ride. Can we post pictures?"

Hope's festive mood immediately crashed. "We'll take pictures," she promised. "But I don't think we should post them until the sheriff catches the bad men."

Emi's upper lip trembled, and Hope feared a complete meltdown was coming. Her little girl was usually well-behaved, but Hope would challenge anyone who expected better of Emi after all she'd been through. She was frankly glad to see Emi complaining. It was a sign of her resilience.

"So, which one was today—the snowball fight or the tree?" Sarah asked, and Hope smiled her gratitude.

Emi didn't have to think twice. "Today is cut down and decorate a Christmas tree."

"We can certainly do that," Sarah responded enthusiastically.

"But you already have a Christmas tree," Emi said sadly.

"This is a Christmas tree ranch—we have lots of trees, don't we, Ian? And I have an idea for a special tree. Maybe we could dig one up and put it in a bucket by the side of the porch. We can decorate it with treats for the birds and squirrels. And then you can watch from the window when they come eat it. How does that sound?"

Emi clapped her hands in glee. "When can we go? Can we go now?"

Hope was thrilled by Emi's joy until she noticed the matching looks of concern on Ian's and Nancy's faces.

As they started to clear the table, Hope overheard Ian trying to dissuade his mother, but she was having none of it. "It will just have to be your job to keep her safe."

Ian loved his mother dearly, and respected her always, but there were times like now that he wished she could back down and respect his expertise. She always saw the best in everyone and had a hard time accepting evil in the world. He loved that about her, but after what he'd endured with Hope and Emi the past few days, taking this kind of risk felt foolhardy, even if it was hard to resist the chance to make Emi smile.

*It will just have to be your job to keep her safe.* How did his own mother not understand how harsh those words were to him? He'd been unable to save his wife and son despite all the best medical care. Yet she tossed off the admonition like it was a matter of choice.

Emi's laughter pulled him from his deteriorating thoughts, and even in his harsh mood, he had to admit he found her charm engaging. Nancy had brought the sleigh around to indulge Emi so they could ride over to the Christmas tree sector of the farm, but Emi was currently giggling

her way through a reindeer photo shoot. Her unadulterated
joy was enough to momentarily lighten Ian's heart.

"Look, Mommy, he likes me." Emi had nuzzled her face
against the reindeer's.

Ian stepped forward. "Why don't you give me your
phone?" he suggested to Hope. "I'll snap a mother-daugh-
ter photo—one on each side of Splasher. You can save it
for reindeer games day."

He took a few candid shots, some of them quite silly,
and then he aimed for capturing a tender moment between
mother and daughter. From behind the safety of the camera,
he could indulge himself and study Hope as she was only
with Emi—a vision of loveliness and maternal perfection.

The thought jolted him. He hadn't meant to be compar-
ing her to his late wife, but he realized that every time he
watched her snuggle with Emi or laugh with her, a dart of
resentment pricked him. This was what he'd lost.

*It will just have to be your job to keep her safe.*

Yes, it was, and he was taking no unavoidable chances.

Photo shoot over, Ian bundled them all into the sleigh.
His mother and father had chosen to follow in the warm
truck, so Ian sat in back with Hope and Emi while Nancy
drove.

Emi was chattering on about the reindeer and Christmas
trees so fast that his head was spinning. She'd sure come
out of her shell in the past few hours.

"So, tell me about this reindeer-games day," he prompted
Hope. "What does it mean for the thousands of people who
haven't just been rescued by reindeer?"

Hope laughed lightly, and Ian found himself transfixed.
Emi wasn't the only one who was showing her true per-
sonality.

"The platform has dozens of suggestions from pin-the-red-nose-on-the-reindeer, to a reindeer-race contest which basically is a traditional three-legged race, but wearing antler hats. We've got reindeer-shaped-food recipes and sing-alongs with reindeer-themed songs. You'd be surprised how many of those there are. There are virtual links to so many possibilities—online reindeer games that our coders developed, virtual reality trips to a reindeer rescue and videos to learn about reindeer and virtually adopt one."

Ian listened in awe as her voice grew more animated with every word. "You did all of this?"

Hope blushed adorably. "Oh, no. I had lots of help. I developed the concept, but our coders did all the work."

Ian just shook his head in amazement. "It's very creative. No wonder Emi is so excited. But how does Christmas Village tie in?"

"It doesn't. Not really. Emi saw an ad for it on television and couldn't stop talking about how many days of the activities she could fill in there. Unfortunately, by the time she discovered it, every ticket was sold out."

"I'm sensing there's a *but*…"

Hope ducked her head, and he watched her take a deep breath. Some of the glimmer had worn off her voice when she spoke again. "The day of the attack, Steve surprised her with tickets. Somehow, he had gotten a pair and found us lodging. That's why he was in my office just before the attackers came in—to give us the tickets and make me leave early."

Ian noticed the shadow cross her face. "What?"

She shrugged. "Maybe it's nothing, but like I told you in the cave, I picked up on something being off. He was really eager to get me out of the office."

All fun fell away, and Ian went on alert. "You think he knew something was going to happen?"

"Maybe? No." She shook her head. "That wouldn't make sense. How would he know we were going to be attacked?"

Ian didn't respond right away. He wasn't sure what to do with the information, but he wasn't going to ignore a possible clue. "I don't want to discuss it in front of Emi," he murmured, "but we should talk to Nancy when we get back. This is her area of expertise. Not mine."

The sleigh pulled up behind the entrance to the tree lot, and Ian drew in a sharp breath. This was even worse than he'd feared. The end of the storm must have drawn out all the tree shoppers. Families eager to cut down their perfect tree swarmed the entranceway armed with axes and saws. Ian studied every adult face, not willing to overlook any possible threat.

He turned to Hope. "I should have done this before, but we need to exchange phone numbers—just in case we get separated," he added, trying to make it sound a little less ominous.

Once they had done that, Nancy hustled Emi and Hope around to the back where local volunteers were doling out steaming mugs of cocoa.

"This is like something straight out of Twelve Days 'til Christmas," Hope pronounced, her voice full of delight. Her joy was infectious, and Ian found himself smiling even as he trailed behind keeping watch.

"All of this is Ian's pet project," Nancy replied. "He recruits all these volunteers to make this sale a huge success for the veterans' center's programs."

As Ian listened to Nancy sing his praises, he was reminded of all the trees that had burned with the truck. Insurance would cover the truck, and he could never regret stepping in to rescue Hope and Emi, but the trees were undeniably a big loss. He should be happy about the crowds today, because they'd help make up some of the replacement cost. And he would be happy—but he wouldn't let down his guard.

"Ian, we're heading back to the live-tree section," Nancy called.

Ian nodded. "Right behind you." He was probably being overly cautious. There was no reason for the gunmen who had chased them to expect Hope to be at a Christmas tree sale. And yet, concern lingered. They'd been uncanny in their ability to track her so far.

Ian hurried to keep up as Emi skipped on ahead and Hope and Nancy quickened their pace to keep up.

"Stay with us, Em," Hope called, but Emi was delightedly running from tree to tree, sniffing the snow-laden pine branches.

"It smells like Christmas, Mommy."

Hope bent down to sniff the branch, and Ian watched in amusement as she purposely buried her nose in the snowy branch. When she lifted her head, she smiled at Emi.

"You're right," she agreed.

Emi started giggling, and Hope deadpanned. "What's wrong?"

Emi laughed even harder and pointed at her nose.

Hope turned to Ian, a mischievous grin on her face. "Do you see something wrong with my face?"

Ian struck a thoughtful pose and pretended to study her. "Hmm. I think your face is quite…" *Lovely*, his heart suggested. *Perfect*. "Quite cold," he finished lamely.

Emi giggled harder.

"But you know," he continued, "I think Emi's face is missing something." He scooped a handful of snow off the branch and made a fluffy snowball. "You wanted a snowball fight, didn't you?" With exaggerated steps he headed toward Emi, who ran and hid behind her mother.

Ian handed off the snowball to Hope, who turned and plopped it on Emi's nose, inducing a fit of laughter. Then she scooped another handful and advanced on Ian.

"Emi's not the only one missing something."

Before Ian had time to realize what was happening, she'd lobbed it right into his face.

Sputtering with surprise and delight, Ian bent down and grabbed another handful, which he didn't even bother to shape before tossing it at Hope.

When she looked up at him with joy shining in her eyes, something flipped in his heart. Her lashes were sparkling with the powdery snow. Her cheeks glowed red from the exertion, and she looked so relaxed and happy that she stole his breath away.

Without conscious thought, Ian stepped toward her and gently brushed the snow from her face with his gloved fingertips. His fingers stilled, and he was entranced, only vaguely hearing Nancy call Emi to check out a special tree.

Her insistent voice finally penetrated his haze, and he hastily stepped back, tripping over a tree in the process. As he fell backward, landing flat on his back in the snow, he could see Hope laughing merrily, but he also saw a glimmer of something dangerous in her eyes, something he'd vowed never to allow again.

He jumped up and vigorously brushed the snow from his coat. "We'd better go catch up with Nance. I don't want them getting too far ahead of us."

Hope's face shuttered, and despite the sting, Ian assured himself that it was for the best.

Hope hurried forward to catch up with her daughter and Nancy, while Ian followed behind at a safe distance, chastising himself for getting caught up in fun and letting down his guard. He carefully scanned the back lot and went on alert when he spied a person behind the trees. But seconds later a woman and child called out to the man, and he smiled and pointed to a tree.

Just another family shopping for trees, Ian decided, but it served as a reminder that he couldn't allow himself to get caught up in Hope's little family. He'd lost the right to have his own family when his wife and son died. His only role was to protect Hope and Emi. And he'd keep reminding himself of that as often as necessary.

"Emi, Emi, where are you?"

The fear in Hope's voice sent Ian running ahead until he caught up to her. "What happened?"

"We were looking at trees," Hope responded, panic rising in her voice. She ran behind a tree to look at something. "I called to her to come back, but suddenly she wasn't there."

Fear clogged Ian's throat. While he'd been musing about families, Emi had gone missing. "Where's Nancy?"

"She went running through the trees to look for her."

Ian considered what to do. "The best plan would be for you to stay here in case Emi just got lost and comes back. But I don't want to leave you alone. Nancy should have stayed with you, but come, we'll look together."

"No. You're right. I'll wait here. I'll be fine."

Ian knew he couldn't take the time to argue with her. Every passing second meant Emi could be farther and farther away—either lost or taken.

"Call me immediately if she comes back or if anything scares you."

"Just find my daughter. Nothing scares me as much as losing her."

# TEN

Ian raced through the trees, Hope's words urging him on. Images of Emi laughing with the reindeer raced through his mind. He could not let anything happen to this little girl.

"Mr. Ian!"

For a moment Ian thought he was hallucinating, but when he swung around, he saw Emi sitting on the ground with tears streaming down her face.

"Emi, what happened?"

She hung her head. "Don't be mad."

Ian deliberately lowered his voice. "I'm not mad at all. Your mama and Nancy and I were so worried. Why did you run off?"

She looked up at him, wide blue eyes still shimmering, but now with joy. "I saw a bunny. I tried to get closer, but he ran away. I followed him, but he ran more, and then… then I got lost."

Ian swallowed back all the fears, all the guilt, and just picked her up in his arms. "How about we call your mommy and tell her I'm bringing you back?"

Ian pulled out his phone and dialed. When he heard Hope's worried voice, he said, "I have someone here who wants to talk to her mommy." He felt her gush of relief as he handed the phone to Emi.

"I'm sorry, Mommy. I chased a bunny, but he got away and I got lost, but Mr. Ian found me."

Ian couldn't make out Hope's words, but as he watched Emi's reaction, he was struck again at how great a mother Hope was.

After a few minutes, Emi passed the phone back to him. "Mommy wants to talk to you."

Ian took the phone and cradled it by his ear to hear as he trudged through the snow with Emi in his arms. "Hope, hey. Emi's safe with me. We're heading back now."

There was no answer, so Ian pulled back to look at the phone. It showed the seconds continuing to tick on the call. "Hope?"

"Ian, help!"

Hope's scream through the phone triggered the most paralyzing fear Ian had ever known.

"Hope, what's happening?"

Only the sounds of a struggle came through the phone. Ian looked down at the young child in his arms and faced an impossible choice. With every cell in his body, he wanted to run after Hope and rescue her, but he was responsible for her child. Ian could feel Emi's trembling body, and in that instance, he knew he would do anything to help this frightened girl who had endured way more than any child should in the past few days.

"I need you to hold tight, okay? I'm going to bring you to Nancy and then help your mommy."

Emi nodded against his shoulder and snuggled into his arms in a way that left Ian breathless. He fought back against the longing to feel his own child's arms around him, and concentrated instead on calling Nancy. *Pick up*, he mentally begged, but the phone rang through to voice-mail. He could only pray she was rescuing Hope.

As he reached the edge of the sale yard, Ian spied his mother volunteering on the hot cocoa line and called to her. She looked up and must have registered the panic on his face, because she instantly set the ladle down and bustled toward him.

"Emi got lost and needs to be watched with an eagle eye. I have to go find Hope."

His mother took Emi from her arms and didn't ask questions. She just touched his arm and whispered, "I'll pray."

Her mother's touch centered him, and Ian nodded his thanks. "Have you seen Nancy?"

"Last I saw, she and Hope were searching for this one back by the taller trees."

Hope struggled against the man whose arms held her tightly. His gloved hand covered her mouth, and he hissed in her ear, "If you ever want to see that pretty little girl of yours again, you'll stop fighting and come quietly."

Hope stopped struggling at his words. Emi was safe with Ian, but that also meant there was no one to help her, since she and Nancy had separated. She would have to rescue herself. That required a clear head rather than panic. Step one: let him think he'd scared her. She forced her entire body to calm so he'd believe she was cooperating.

"That's better," he muttered.

"What do you want with me?" Hope tried to ask, but his hand was too tight against her mouth, and nothing but garbled sounds emerged.

She fought back against the mind-numbing fear and focused on the man and the way he was holding her. He had one arm wrapped around her neck with his hand over her mouth. The other hand was clutching her left arm as he dragged her backward. That left her right hand free, and because she had taken off her gloves to answer her phone, it wasn't encumbered.

She formulated her plan and then mentally counted backward from three. *Two. One.* She took a deep breath in through her nose, and then made her entire body go limp in his arms. The sudden shift threw him off balance, and she reached up with her free hand to claw at the inside of his wrist where his jacket met his glove.

He groaned in pain, and his hand slipped away from her mouth long enough for her to let out a piercing scream.

"That was a stupid move," the man grunted as he grappled to regain control, but Hope wasn't giving up so easily. She twisted in his grip and raised her hand to his head. She grabbed at his knit cap trying to grasp his hair.

He yanked her arm hard and his hat came off in her hand, exposing a tattoo that snaked up the side of his neck and into his hairline. While her body fought to escape, Hope made her mind focus on memorizing the design of intertwined letters and lines.

He twirled her around and for one terrifying moment, their eyes met. Hope shivered at the darkness that stared back at her. She forced herself to hold his gaze as she put all her force into her leg and kneed him.

He fell back with a howl. Hope turned to flee, and her heart lifted at the sight of Ian emerging through the trees. She wanted to run straight into his arms, but the man had run off through the trees, so instead she called, "Help me! We can't let him get away."

Knowing Ian would follow, she turned and chased the man who moments before had tried to kidnap her. The snow was deeper here, and though that made running more difficult, it was easy to follow his footprints.

Ian easily caught up. He ran beside her long enough to

check that she was okay, and then he sprinted ahead. Hope wasn't used to running long distances and between the abduction attempt and the stress of the past few days, she felt her energy fading quickly. She slowed to a light jog and then to a walk, praying that Ian could capture him.

The sound of a car engine starting up dashed that hope, and she struggled to summon the energy to keep going. When she finally broke through the last of the Christmas tree rows, she saw Ian trudging back up the road as a truck disappeared in the distance.

When he saw her, he ran forward and quickly closed the distance between them. He opened his arms, and Hope walked straight into them, collapsing against the strength of him as his arms wrapped around her. *Safe.* She was safe.

All the trauma caught up with her, and she started shivering uncontrollably.

"You're okay, I've got you. You're safe," Ian murmured as he tightened his comforting embrace.

For a few moments, Hope just let herself rest against him, drawing strength from him, trying to ease the anxiety that had her entire body trembling. Eventually, she eased back so she could look up at him. "Emi?"

She tried to form the words to ask where her baby was, but his face was so close, and the expression in his eyes so kind and comforting. She focused on them, trying to erase the fear she'd felt staring into the unfathomable darkness of her abductor's eyes.

Ian reached up to brush some snow from her hair, and his gentle touch was too much. She had to close her eyes against a rush of emotion.

"Emi is with my mother. Let me know when you can walk," he murmured. "I don't know where Nancy is or I'd call her to help."

Hope hung her head. "I tried to find her. I know you said to wait," she added in a rush. "But I was so scared, and it seemed foolish to do nothing when we could cover more ground if I was looking too." She looked up at him again. "I was wrong not to listen to you."

Ian laughed softly. "How hard was that to say?"

Hope pulled back out of his arms and joined in his laughter. "Not as hard as it would have been if you hadn't just rescued me."

"Oh, I don't get any credit for that," Ian said. "From what I could see, you had it all taken care of before I even got here."

Hope felt the admiration in his voice and her heart lightened. "I tried to be smart, not scared." Her fear was receding under his steady presence.

"Smart is always good," he replied. "But healthy fear is important too."

She nodded. "I promise to follow your directions from now on."

His laugh was hearty this time. "That sounds like something the teacher might force you to write fifty times on the board as punishment." His voice grew serious. "It's not something I want to be right about, but if anything, this proved these men know no boundaries and aren't giving up."

Hope shuddered. "What am I going to do?"

He tilted her chin with a gentle fingertip until she met his gaze again. "First thing is to accept you're not alone. I will not leave you until this is completely over, and you and Emi can have your life again."

Hope nodded, thankful for his assurance, but a chasm opened in her heart at his final words. Once this was over, he'd be gone from her life. That thought disturbed her much more than it should.

Ian wrapped his arm around her shoulders. "Let's go find Nancy and Emi. And you can tell me what just happened."

Hope absorbed the comfort of his embrace as she tried to find the words to explain how she'd been caught unawares.

"Nancy and I separated, and I was checking behind the trees. I saw some other people in the distance, but all of a sudden there was an arm around my neck pulling me back behind the trees." She shivered at the memory. "He told me if I ever wanted to see my little girl again, that I had to go with him."

Ian hugged her a little tighter. "I'm sorry. That must have been terrifying."

Hope grinned up at him. "He'd never understand, obviously, but those were fighting words to a mother. He unleashed mama bear. I pretended to go along, but only until I could outsmart him. You appeared right after I broke away."

Hope fell silent. She didn't want to admit to Ian what had made her miss the threat until it was too late. She'd seen a couple, and that had triggered memories of a time when she was young and happy. Once, she had been part of a couple like that, shopping for their first tree right after she'd found out she was pregnant with Emi. Her heart had been so full of hope, so filled to bursting with joy that she was building the family she'd always wanted.

Her parents had been older and occupied with their careers. They'd never said so, but she'd always suspected she was a surprise. A welcome one, but a gift they weren't quite sure what to do with. They'd passed away within a year of each other shortly before she'd married Keith. In the past year, she'd sometimes wondered if maybe she'd been so quick to marry him to recapture the family she had lost.

After Ian called to say he'd found Emi, she'd lost herself

in thoughts about how everything had fallen apart. Then the man grabbed her.

"Hope? Earth to Hope?"

She bolted alert and laughed. "That's what I'm always saying to Emi." Her face fell as she remembered the last time she'd said it… Steve had just walked into her office. "I need to call the hospital again and check on Steve."

If Ian was surprised by her abrupt change of topic, he didn't show it.

"Okay, but I think there's someone who's waiting to see you."

Hope looked up, surprised to see they were already back at the yard. Emi was waving at her, and nothing had ever looked so wonderful. She pulled away from Ian and ran toward her little girl and scooped her up in a hug. "I am never letting you out of my sight again," she whispered as Emi returned the hug.

# ELEVEN

Emi led Hope to where Ian's mother was waiting by a truck filled with the potted trees. Sarah reached up to give Hope a warm hug.

"Don't tell Ian I said so, but he was right. We're going to take these trees back to my crafting barn and work on them inside."

Hope laughed. "I just told him he was right that Nancy and I should have stayed together."

His mother chuckled. "All the more reason for me not to say it. His head will get too big." She turned to Emi. "What do you say, are you ready to help me make these trees into a feast for the birds and squirrels?"

Emi looked at her shyly. "Can Mommy help?"

"Of course. The more the merrier. And when we're done, we'll go back to the kitchen and bake those cookies you missed out on. How does that sound?"

Emi beamed and looked to her mother for approval. Honestly, Hope thought it sounded exhausting. All she wanted to do was curl up next to a fire and sleep. She stifled a yawn and tried to inject some enthusiasm into her voice. "Sounds like a great plan."

As they climbed into the truck, she looked around for Nancy and Ian. They were standing by the sleigh, and it

looked like Nancy was on the receiving end of all the re-
bukes Ian had spared her. She needed to apologize. It had
been her idea after all.

"Don't mind them," Sarah commented in a stage whisper.
"They've been having spats like that since they could talk."

Ian and Nancy turned and waved. "I heard that," Ian
called.

"Then stop yelling at your sister and come help us get
these trees back to the barn."

"Yes, ma'am."

Nancy gave her brother a quick hug before she climbed
up in the sleigh and headed back to the reindeer barn. Ian
strode over and climbed into the back of the truck.

When they arrived at the barn, Hope was amazed yet
again. The door rolled back to reveal what looked like Sarah's personal craft store.

"Wow! I've never seen anything like this," she exclaimed.

"My mother is a one-woman craft army," Ian explained.
"All those wreaths and bouquets and decorations you saw
for sale at the tree lot—she made all of those to support
the veterans' center."

"Stop your nonsense," Sarah tsked, coming up behind
them. "We have work to do."

She quickly set Emi and Hope to work making edible
ornaments out of birdseed. Once the cakes were formed,
Emi got to work using an assortment of cookie cutters, but
Hope needed to stand and stretch.

She headed to a remote corner of the barn and tried once
again to reach the hospital. She explained that she was
Steve's closest living relation—true even if their relationship was friendship. Unfortunately, the nurse on duty was
a stickler for rules and wouldn't even confirm that Steve

was there. But since the operator had put her through to a floor, Hope decided he must be. She breathed a sigh. If he was in the hospital, that meant that he was at least alive. Ian had promised to bring her to the sheriff tomorrow, so she would beg to stop by the hospital and check for herself.

Nancy had returned from the reindeer barn and was standing guard near the door with Ian. Hope hurried in their direction, but as she drew close, she could overhear snippets of their conversation.

"Stop blaming yourself, Ian."

"They almost got her," Ian replied. "She could have been kidnapped."

"But she wasn't." Nancy crossed her arms as she faced her brother. "You said yourself that she did a fine job of fighting him off. And you got there as quickly as you could."

"Not fast enough to catch him," Ian replied as he paced across the room.

"No, because you were off rescuing her daughter."

"Who should never have been allowed to wander away in the first place."

Nancy walked up to him and put a hand on each shoulder. "Listen to yourself, Ian. Something else is driving this reaction. You have nothing to feel guilty about."

He shook her off and turned away, but Nancy followed, unaware of Hope's approach.

"She's a child. She wandered off chasing a rabbit. Children do that kind of thing. Do you know how many calls law enforcement gets for things like this? It's nerve-wracking for the parents, but it's okay. She was fine."

"Nancy is right." Hope walked into the scene feeling very much like she she'd interrupted something she didn't really understand but needed to correct. "All of this is on me. If I hadn't stowed away in your truck, you and your family wouldn't even have been involved. But now I've brought all of this on you. If anyone is at fault here, it's me. I let Emi wander away, and if I had been more alert, that man never would have had a chance to grab me."

"Nope, nothing like Shelby," Nancy muttered, and somehow Hope felt that was a compliment.

"I'm sorry you took the blame too, Nancy. This is all on me." She turned and glared at Ian. "Your sister did nothing wrong and neither did you." Then, deciding it was time to defuse the tension, Hope turned to both of them. "I'm very sorry I involved you, but you need to know we may never be able to drag Emi out of here. She's hooked."

Nancy laughed. "You've probably realized by now that my mother's life goal was to be Mrs. Claus. She'll be happy to welcome Elf Emi into the fold."

Hope laughed and was surprised to realize how much steadier she felt. "Your family is amazing."

Nancy shrugged. "We've got our good days. But we're just like everyone else—human." She stopped and stared at Ian, "And fallible."

Then Nancy got serious. "This afternoon happened, and we have to learn from it and do better. So, let's talk." She waved Hope over to a sofa and chairs that created a seating area in an alcove by the barn door.

Ian had been silent since Hope's speech, but in what seemed a gesture of reconciliation, he spoke. "There's coffee or tea if you'd like something to drink."

Hope's calm had fled with Nancy's invitation to talk, so she decided a cup of something hot to hold would be a good idea. "Thank you. Coffee would be great. I could use the caffeine boost. I'm not much of an Elf Hope, I'm afraid."

Nancy laughed. "Hang around my mother long enough and you won't have a choice."

As Hope waited for Ian to bring over the coffee, she couldn't help but wish she would have a chance to spend time with his mom. Nancy might think her family was like everyone else, but as an outsider who'd never had anything like this, Hope knew they were truly special.

Ian handed her a mug of steaming coffee and set cream and sugar on the end table before settling onto the sofa across from her.

"No coffee for Nancy?"

Nancy laughed again. "He's not punishing me. I don't drink it unless I'm on duty." She cleared her throat, and in a voice low enough for just the three of them to hear, began to speak. "After this, we have to acknowledge that the attack at your office was most likely an attempt to kidnap you. Can you think of any idea why?"

Hope was truly shaken hearing Nancy utter the words. Even though she'd come to the same conclusion, it was particularly rattling to hear it confirmed by someone in law enforcement. "I've wracked my brain, but I have no clue."

Nancy persisted. "Is there anything in your life that you can think of that would be a reason people would want something from you?"

Hope thought hard. "Not really. As I told Ian, I live a pretty simple life. When my husband died, Emi and I moved here to take the job with Steve's company. Basically, I work, I take Emi to school, I sleep. Wash and repeat. Add in buy groceries once a week. There's absolutely nothing special about me or my life."

Ian begged to differ. After knowing Hope for slightly less than two days, he already knew there was a lot about her that was special. She was an outstanding mother, a dedicated and creative worker, beautiful, kind, courageous... He caught himself before he got too carried away.

Hope had covered everything about her current life, but there was a glaring question that needed to be asked. He and Nancy had spoken about it earlier. Ian couldn't figure out how to broach the topic of her husband, so he surreptitiously nodded the okay to Nancy.

She picked up on it right away. "Hope, this is delicate, and I know it's extremely personal, but I have to ask. What about your husband? How did he die? Could that have anything to do with this?"

Ian's heart ached as he watched Hope's whole body shrink in on itself, a transformation that deeply troubled him.

"My husband was having an affair. He died in Los Angeles, in a car accident with the woman he'd gone to see."

Her words were robotic, as if she were repeating well-rehearsed lines that relayed the facts and required no emotion. Silence hung heavy in the cold barn air. Ian had no idea what to say to that. He was drowning in all the hurt that swam in her eyes.

Nancy's voice, when she picked up, was gentler than he'd ever heard it. "The woman, did she have family? Could it be someone bent on revenge?"

Hope looked up, horror replacing the despair in her eyes. "I don't know." She hung her head, and her voice was barely audible. "To be honest, I was in such shock at the news that I never even inquired if she had family."

"Do you know her name?"

Watching Hope process that question, Ian suspected that the name haunted her.

"Susan."

She said it so quietly that Ian had to struggle to hear the name, but the pain behind it rang clear.

"I know it's a long shot, but if you can give me a last name, I'll have my people look into it," Nancy assured them. "Moving on, what about work? Any problems there?"

"No."

Ian noted that Hope appeared on steadier ground talking about work.

"Steve has been very successful. The company is doing well. And the program I told you about at lunch, it has been extremely profitable."

"Would anyone have issues with that?"

"Why would anyone have a problem with us being successful?" Hope looked genuinely confused by the notion.

Nancy's eyes widened. "Because people can be that way. Any disgruntled employees? Someone who got fired?"

Hope shook her head vehemently. "Not a chance. Steve is one of those bosses who believes in rewarding his employees for their efforts. Everyone got a really nice bonus when the app crossed a million downloads and then an even nicer one when it hit ten million."

"Ten million?" Nancy questioned. "That's a lot of downloads."

Ian swallowed a laugh at his sister's understatement.

"I'll bring it to our tech guys and see if they have any thoughts," she added.

"If there's anything to do with the finances of the company, I don't know why they'd want me. I'm just the design and marketing person. I have nothing to do with money. You'd need to talk to Steve about that. But we can't do that. I called the hospital. They won't tell me anything, but I got the impression he *is* there." She thought a bit more. "Maybe our accountant can help."

"I'll check with the hospital and reach out to the head of accounting. But tell me about your relationship with Steve," Nancy prompted.

Hope released a deep sigh, and Ian could see the toll this conversation was taking on her. She looked on the verge of collapse. He loved his sister, and knew she was an excellent agent, but Hope needed a break, so he spoke up.

"It looks like Mom and Emi are finishing up. Why don't we head back to the house, get Hope something to eat, distract Emi, and then we can talk more."

Nancy looked like she wanted to protest but thought better of it. "Okay."

Once they were back at the house, his mother took charge as Ian had hoped. She edged Nancy aside and prepared a cup of hot tea and a scone for Hope.

When Hope was settled by the fireplace, and Emi and his mother were up to their elbows in flour and sugar and out of hearing range, Nancy dove right back in with questions that came fast and furious.

Ian, who was sitting beside Hope on the sofa, interrupted. "This is my sister the hard-nosed Fed. Don't let her overwhelm you."

Hope laid a hand on his arm. "It's fine. I can take the hard questions if answering them will help solve this problem and stop the danger."

Ian relented. He knew they were both right, and frankly he wasn't sure where this strong need to protect Hope came from. He could tell himself it was just because he'd witnessed all she'd survived these last few days, but that wouldn't be honest. Deep inside he knew it was something more, something he was feeling that he couldn't allow to develop.

He abruptly stood and paced to the window. As he lis-

tened to Hope's soft voice, he couldn't help but be aware
of every nuance in her words.

"I told Ian a condensed version of this. Steve and I met
in college. My computer crashed when I was in the middle
of an important project. I was on the verge of hysterics,
but someone told me there were these two guys who were
wizards at anything related to computers. I found them and
threw myself on their mercy."

She paused and took a sip of her tea, but he sensed she
needed the moment to compose herself more than she
needed the beverage.

"Steve was one of those guys." She bit her lip and swallowed hard. "My future husband was the other. We clicked
and became a trio of sorts. Steve always had a different
girlfriend, but the three of us were tight as thieves. When
we graduated, they went on to form a business, Keith and I
married and life went on pretty much the same. For a time."

Her pause this time was longer and seemed heavier.

"I should have realized something was off when Keith
started traveling more. Afterward, I berated myself for a
long time, wondering what I could have done differently,
wondering if the outcome would have been different if I'd
noticed his dissatisfaction sooner."

She visibly shook herself. "I'm sorry. I shouldn't have
shared that. My failures as a wife have nothing to do with
this." She swiped at a tear. "I really have no idea why anyone would be after me."

Ian ground his fists in his pocket as he listened to the
pain that poured out of every word. He understood all too
well what it felt like to be left behind. To have so many
questions and no way to get answers. To have to go on living when the doubt and grief swamped you.

"So, this is the rest of my sad story, in case you can find

any meaning in it," Hope continued. "After Keith died, I was in a pretty bad place—adrift. I had a young child, no money, no ideas, and frankly I was drowning. Steve threw me a lifeline. He relocated the company here to Colorado and offered me the marketing job. That had been my major in college and I'd helped them out when they were getting started—until Emi was born. By then the company was doing well enough that we could afford for me to stay home."

Nancy cleared her throat. "I apologize if this is intrusive, but know I'm asking with our goal in mind."

Hope gave a single nod and waited.

"If the business was doing so well, why were you destitute when your husband died?"

Hope buried her face in her hands for a moment before sitting up and stiffening her back. It was all Ian could do not to envelop her in a hug, but he had no right.

When Hope spoke again, there was a bitterness he hadn't heard before. "Apparently my husband had developed a taste for the good things in life. He'd wiped out our accounts. I suppose supporting your family while entertaining another woman can do that to you, regardless of your business success."

"Did he have ownership in the company?"

"Initially, when they founded the business, yes. But I found out that Steve bought out most of his shares. We've never spoken of it, but I think Steve knew more than he let on, and I think he felt guilty about how it left me." She wrapped her arms across her chest and hugged them close. "It was never his fault. I didn't blame him."

Nancy sat back, and Ian read the frustration on her face. "I'll do some digging, see what I can find out." She looked at her phone and sighed. "I spoke to the sheriff while you were moving up here from the barn."

"Did he know anything about what happened?"

"No, different sheriff. Our ranch is in a different county than your office. I explained what happened out at the lot today and connected it to the other events. He said he would check in with law enforcement investigating the events at your office, but in the meantime, he'd send a deputy out to investigate the tree lot. I'm afraid he's going to want to talk to you. I just got a text that he's down by the road, so I'll meet him."

Ian knew Nancy had been right to call the sheriff, but right now he didn't appreciate her bringing more difficulty to Hope. Then his sister surprised him.

Nancy walked over to the sofa and sat in the spot Ian had vacated. She grasped both of Hope's hands in hers and said the words that had been burning in Ian's heart.

"Don't ever consider yourself a failure. He was the one who broke his vows. Don't waste any time worrying about it." She hung her head a moment. "I get that it's hard when you have unanswered questions." Nancy's voice cracked. "But you have made a new life for yourself and your beautiful little girl. Celebrate that. Ian and I will do everything in our power to help you reclaim it. Right, little brother?"

Ian wanted to go hug his sister tight, but he knew she'd resent it, so he joked instead. "In this family we have learned to always follow Nancy's directions."

# TWELVE

The visit to the sheriff's office the next morning frustrated Hope. She'd endured another humiliating round of the same questions the deputy had asked the previous evening, and received nothing in return. No news about the attack, and the only information she had about Steve came from Nancy's sources. He was in a medically induced coma. His close friend, Helen, was with him—no surprise there. Helen was his admin and could talk her way into anything—but no other visitors were allowed.

Hope struggled with that as they drove back to the ranch. More than almost anything, she wanted to be the one by his side. But she had to stay with Emi, because the attack yesterday proved they were still in danger from an unknown source.

"Did you know that reindeers' eyes change color?"

Emi's cheerful voice broke into Hope's thoughts. "What, sweetie?"

Emi held up the book she was reading. "Nancy gave me this book about reindeer. It says their eyes are gold in the summer but turn blue in the winter."

"That's interesting," Hope replied. "What else did you learn?"

"That they have hairy noses and their hooves are like snow shovels."

Emi turned back to her book, reading and occasionally sharing reindeer trivia. Hope stared out the window at the passing scenery and mined her memories for anything that would explain the trouble they were in.

Eventually the rhythm of the car lulled Emi to sleep. Hope carefully removed the book from her lap. Since Ian was driving and Nancy was doing work, Hope opened her phone to check her own work email.

Immediately, a text message popped up. A scream rose in her throat, but she swallowed the sound as she felt Emi shift beside her.

"What's wrong?" Ian asked.

"I just got a text message. It's a photo. Here." She handed the phone to Nancy, not willing to risk Emi overhearing her describe it. The photo showed them at the tree lot. There was a sniper's crosshairs superimposed on Emi's head. Below the image was a demand.

Pay up or you'll pay a higher price.

Hope started to shake uncontrollably. "What does this mean? How am I supposed to pay if I don't know who or what this is?"

Ian focused on the demand. "We have to presume this is connected to the attack at your workplace. It must involve Steve. Are you sure you don't know anything?"

"I don't." Frustration laced with fear in her voice. "And we can't ask him if he's in a coma."

"Is there anyone else you could ask?"

"Helen. She's his dear friend as well as his admin. If anyone knows anything, she would."

Nancy handed her phone back and Hope called, but it went straight to voicemail. She left a message begging Helen to reply immediately. "I'll email her and explain in case she tries to contact me when we aren't in range."

Hope opened her work email and was immediately overwhelmed with hundreds of company emails. Most were from coworkers checking on her and expressing condolences. Guilt swamped her. She'd been so busy trying to stay alive that she hadn't even thought about her coworkers' reactions.

She clicked on her important-email tab, and her heart thudded as she saw one from Steve. She opened it and scanned through, but her hands were trembling so badly she could barely hold the phone. She handed it to Nancy again. "You read it."

Nancy started to read aloud.

"Hope, if you are reading this, I'm probably in trouble. Our company has been threatened. I have it under control, but this is my backup plan. I'm composing this email so you'll have all the facts, but each day I'll reschedule it. You'll only receive it if I have been unable to access my email for 24 hours. Not to be excessively dramatic, but if you are reading this, something (most likely very bad) has happened to me.

Two months ago, when Twelve Days 'til Christmas was climbing the charts and being hailed as the marketing coup and top app of the season, I received an anonymous threat. It was a ransomware demand. I didn't take it seriously, so what followed falls squarely on my shoulders.

I was not worried.

I should have been.

Last week, I received the most serious demand yet. If I do not pay the asking price (which has now quadrupled from the original outrageous demand), they will hold their own grand finale and reveal that they have stolen all the data from our subscribers and will put it up for sale on the dark web."

Nancy stopped reading and shot Ian a look.

"Is that it?" Hope prompted.

"No." She read on.

"Call me arrogant (and you will because you know me so well), but I was not willing to surrender our hard-earned money to these criminals. I decided to dig into the app and find out how they found an entry point and if they had stolen our data.

I found a malicious code that makes the app crash. When it does, you have to input your information again to regain access. The link they give within the app is a portal—to their mother ship.

By now you're probably calling me every name in the Greek alphabet and not in a good way. I know I should have sought help, but who better to reverse engineer this than the man who created it in the first place?

Sadly, I must admit that if you're reading this, I've failed. That pains me because it means I have been unable to stop these villains in their plan to release all the private information of our Christmas family. My platform, that was supposed to be a source of comfort and security, is on the verge of becoming every family's cybersecurity nightmare.

I'm sorry."

Silence settled in the car as Nancy finished reading.

Outside a few snowflakes sifted through the air, but inside the tension was thick.

Ian was the first to speak. "First we have to determine if this was actually written by Steve."

Hope swallowed past the lump in her throat. "It sounds like him. *Portal. Mother ship.* Steve geeks out over sci-fi. His first college project was a design that let you travel into the spaceship with the aliens and go on adventures. It was sort of a mashup of all his favorite movies."

Ian laughed. "Steve sounds like an interesting guy."

"He's the best."

Hope caught the look Ian and Nancy exchanged. "No." She shook her head. "Not that way. There was never anything romantic between us. He's my best friend. We connect in some inexplicable platonic way.

"Anyway, this sounds completely like Steve, down to the admission of arrogance. He is very arrogant about his tech ability. He's amazingly creative and just sees things in a way others don't. We need to go see him."

"As you said, he's in a coma," Ian objected.

"People in comas hear things. Maybe if he hears my voice he'll respond."

Ian expressed his unease. "They said no other visitors, and given the text you received, I don't think we can risk it. Helen is there. Let's do a video chat with her when we're back at the ranch. My mother can occupy Emi."

Reluctantly, Hope agreed and sent a text praying Helen would see it and consent to a meeting.

Once they were back at the ranch, Ian had Nancy set up the meeting on a secure server. When they were all gathered, and Helen logged on, he asked Hope to do the introductions and take the lead as they got right to business.

"Helen, can you check your emails?" Hope asked, after she had updated her on the situation. "Steve scheduled an email to me that would be sent if he couldn't access his email. Maybe he sent you one, too."

Helen looked confused and doubtful but she opened her phone. She rolled her eyes. "There are hundreds of them."

"Search for the most recent one from Steve."

A moment passed, then Helen gasped. "You're right."

Ian watched impatiently as Helen read through the email. He wanted to tell her to read it out loud, but from the delicate flush on her cheeks he suspected there were private parts to it that she might not care to share.

When she finally finished, she spoke to Hope in a broken voice. "I can't read it aloud. I'll forward it so you can."

After Hope scanned the email, she spoke to Helen in a tender voice. "Are you sure you're okay with me reading this?"

Helen's eyes glimmered with a mix of tears and something Ian couldn't quite identify. But she nodded. "I don't know if anything he wrote will help, but we have to see. We have to find who did this to him and stop them from hurting families who trusted us. Share whatever you need."

Steel, Ian decided. That's what he'd seen in her eyes. The same solid determination that he'd found in Hope.

Hope read:

"My dearest Helen,
If you are reading this, most likely I am no longer alive."

Hope looked up and smiled bravely at Helen. "You'll get the chance to tell him he's wrong."

Helen choked on a laugh. "That might just kill him."

Ian had a sudden uncomfortable sense of being an outsider. There was nothing surprising in that. These three had worked closely together for years on something that clearly was very personally important to them.

Hope spoke again. "I'm skimming over this. The first part is basically what he wrote in my email, but this is different.

'It was terribly unfair of me to allow you to work these long nights without telling you why we were doing it. I should have explained and taken better advantage of your expertise. I sent a copy of the codes to Hope, but she won't know what they mean.'"

Hope made a disgruntled sound, and Ian thought he heard her muttering under her breath.

She looked at Helen. "What is he talking about? He didn't give me anything. There are no codes in my email." She paused and glanced at Ian. "It gets personal after that, his appreciation of Helen. No need to share it."

Helen shook her head. "Go to the last paragraph."

Hope read.

"I've instructed Victor to pay them before Christmas Eve to stop the release of information. My company, this app are worth nothing compared to the lives that will be ruined."

Silence descended over them, and in it they could hear the faint beep of the machines breathing life into Steve.

"No," Hope whispered. "We can't pay. We can't give in."

Tears streamed down Helen's face. "I understand why you want to fight, Hope. This was your baby as much as Steve's. You poured all of yourself into making it a success. But we can't put the company before the people." Her voice cracked. "Steve wouldn't want that."

Hope waved her off. "That's not it. It's not about me. It's about all the families who trusted us."

She looked at Ian and then at Nancy. "Do you really believe if we pay this ransom that will be the end of it? Will they really just say, *Thanks, we'll trash all the data we stole*?"

Nancy slowly shook her head.

Hope closed her eyes a moment, then faced Ian. "I know you didn't sign on for this, but I have to fight it. I have to stop them."

Nancy laughed. "You don't know my brother. Those are fighting words you just gave him." She looked with love at her brother. "Ian never could stand a bully."

Helen spoke up, and Ian noted that she looked calmer, determined. "What do we do?"

Everyone turned to Nancy.

"I can start," she offered. "I know who to call. There's a Joint Ransomware Task Force. I'll call my friend in IC3— that's our internet crime compliance center. They're the initial contact for anyone who has been a victim of a ransomware attack."

"Helen." Hope's voice softened. "I think you should stay there with Steve." Helen started to protest halfheartedly, but Hope stopped her. "He's in critical condition. Talk to him, see if you can get through to him. We need him, and to be honest, we need his brain working to defeat these guys."

Helen gave a sad smile. "I won't leave his side."

"What am I doing, boss?" Ian teased.

Hope smiled shyly. "Sorry, I just feel really strongly about this."

"And I'll do whatever I can to help."

\* \* \*

After Nancy ended the conference, Hope headed back into the main part of the house. She was happy with their decision, but the sniper's target on Emi's photo preyed on her mind, and she needed time with her little girl.

She stepped into the kitchen and found herself in a Christmas bakeshop. Emi and Sarah had been making cookies, so cinnamon and vanilla scented the air. Emi came rushing toward her covered in butter, flour and sugar. Hope had never in her life been so happy to see anyone. She fell to her knees, and Emi rushed into her arms, giving her a huge hug that felt like love and smelled like everything Christmas.

Hope wrapped her arms around her daughter, and while she hugged Emi tight, she absorbed her surroundings. Ian's mom was wearing her red apron and a smile. The fire in the great room snapped and crackled while soft Christmas music played over the sound system, and the tree was lit with presents piled beneath it. Love filled the air.

This what she had been trying to capture in the community of their app. This sense of family and holiday joy, everything that had been missing from her own life.

It was what Steve had been trying to infuse into a virtual community. Their app was meant to celebrate the holidays with family in every sense—whether biological or found, in real time or virtual. It would be fun for families together, and a haven for those without. It brought love and joy and peace—all the things that Christmas was supposed to be. That's what she was fighting for, and she would do everything in her power to save it from some grinch-like villain.

"Mommy!" Emi squirmed in her embrace. "You didn't tell me you posted my picture with Splasher."

"Hmm, what?"

Emi ran and grabbed her device, waving it at Hope. "I thought we were saving it for reindeer-games day."

Hope glanced at the photo, and her mind froze.

"Emi, I think your mommy needs to talk to Ian and Nancy. Why don't you come help me make a plate of cookies for them?"

Hope roused herself enough to nod her thanks to Sarah. She kept the device and went in search of Ian, because the stakes had just been raised. The photo from the tree lot had been bad enough. But this photo—this was the one Ian took on her phone. And somebody had posted it to her account on the platform.

Ian took one look at Hope's ashen face and jumped to his feet. "What's wrong?"

She held out Emi's device, and he looked at the photo he'd taken of Hope and Emi with the reindeer. "You posted it? Maybe not the wisest—"

"I didn't post it. Emi just showed it to me. Someone hacked my phone."

Hope looked on the verge of collapse, so Ian guided her to the sofa.

Nancy joined them. "Hope, we need to talk about something. Ian and I had just been considering moving to a safe house because of the sniper photo from earlier. This reinforces it. I know you're going to object to my suggestion, but please think carefully about what is best for Emi."

Hope stared at her calmly, but Ian could feel the tremors wracking her body. He rested his hand on her arm to steady her.

"We have a friend. His name is Adam. He's a very good man with a wife and little girl. We think you should send Emi to stay with them until this is resolved."

Hope pulled away from Ian and jumped to her feet. "I can't do that! I can't send my daughter away with a stranger."

"I know he's a stranger to you, but he's a good friend of ours. We wouldn't suggest this unless we felt it was absolutely the best way to keep Emi safe."

"But you're strangers too. I'm sorry, I know that sounds awful after all you've done for me, but she's my baby girl."

Ian came and wrapped his arms around her. "It's because she's your very precious baby girl that we want to protect her from the evil person behind this."

"Why can't I go with her?"

Ian swallowed hard. "Because somehow this is all tied to you." He let that sink in before continuing. "Adam has the most secure house I've ever been in. Emi will be safe with his family, and you will be able to focus on helping us take down the enemy without worrying about them hurting her."

Tears filled Hope's eyes as she stared at them in disbelief.

"Talk to his wife Isabelle, at least," Nancy suggested. "I think you'll feel better about this if you do."

Numb with grief, Hope took the phone. She couldn't believe she was even considering sending her baby away. But as she glanced at the photo on her own phone and remembered the sniper image, she knew she'd make the hard choice, even if it broke her heart.

# THIRTEEN

They decided on Christmas Village for the handoff, hoping that the crowds of tourists would provide anonymity for the switch. The irony of the setting was painfully apparent to Hope as she wandered the streets with Emi before stopping in front of a storefront to chat with Adam. She finally got to visit Christmas Village, only to be separated from her mother.

Ian and Nancy had been right though. The conversation with Isabelle had calmed many of Hope's fears. Meeting Adam now, she immediately knew he would stop at nothing to protect her daughter. Emi was nervous, but Hope pasted on a fake smile and told her it was a great adventure to meet a new friend. Perhaps too wise for her years, Emi put up no fight.

They pulled the switch in a busy restaurant, and once Adam left with her daughter, Hope couldn't hold back her tears any longer. Ian reached across the table and clasped her hands. She knew he only meant to comfort her, and their hands in each other's felt so right that she held on to his strength and let it fill her.

When she thought she could speak without her voice cracking, she lifted her head and looked across at him. Her voice could barely be heard above the clamor of the restaurant, and he leaned in to hear.

"When I was a child, and I read the Narnia books, I always wondered how a mother could send her children away to live with a complete stranger." She shuddered. "Then I grew up and learned about Operation Pied Piper. I understood it on an intellectual level, but it still horrified me." She bowed her head a moment, then looked up at him, her eyes a sheen of tears. "Today, I understand in my heart."

"A mother's sacrifice to save her children. You're very brave, Hope."

She shook her head. "Not brave at all. Just confused and desperate."

"For what it's worth, my mother thinks you made the right choice. And I might be prejudiced, but I think she's one of the all-time greatest mothers, so you should take it as a compliment."

"She thinks that, really?"

Ian smiled. "She feels awful that you were dealt such a bad hand, but she very much admires the way you've handled it."

"It's not like I've had much choice."

"Maybe she's just used to how badly I manage." Ian winked, trying to make her smile.

"The great Ian Fraser is not perfect?" Hope's attempt to rally fell flat.

"Great, huh? I could get used to that."

Hope listened to his joking words, but they rang hollow. Something in the conversation felt off. She couldn't identify what, but something had shifted in his expression when he was talking about a mother's sacrifice. "A penny for your thoughts?"

Ian shook his head, though Hope sensed it was more to clear it than to refuse her.

"Just thinking that enough time has passed. We should get to the house and start searching for this clue," Ian urged.

That had been their other reason for choosing Christmas Village. Thinking of Steve's last-minute gift of the tickets and ski chalet, and his urgent attempt to make her accept, had given Hope the idea that they might find the codes there. It was the only thing she could think of.

They headed out of the restaurant. Soft snowflakes were falling. Combined with the twinkling white lights on every building, they created an air of enchantment. Anger suddenly surged through Hope.

"Penny for *your* thoughts now," Ian teased.

She looked up at him and saw he had picked up on the anger that blazed in her heart.

"I'm just so…so… *Mad* doesn't even come close. Look at this place. Emi was deliriously happy when we got here, but she never even got a chance to enjoy it because these people—whoever they are—have some diabolical plan. What scrooges!"

Ian laughed. "Meet Lioness Hope. The mama who would probably bring down a king if he hurt her little girl."

"Or die trying," Hope replied without thinking.

They both fell silent, the realization that that was entirely possible hitting home with thunderous force.

They got in the car and traveled the short distance to the ski chalet Steve had borrowed for them. Hope's anger resurged as they approached the beautiful log-cabin-style home fully decorated for Christmas. When they entered and found the same holiday wonderland effect inside, tears once again slid down Hope's cheeks.

"Steve had the house decorated for Emi." She swiped away the tears. "He knows her so well. She would have adored spending two weeks here." She smiled wistfully.

"She'd have imagined she was living inside her favorite book, only in Colorado rather than Wisconsin."

Ian came up beside her and drew her into a hug. "I'm sorry. Emi doesn't deserve any of this mess, and neither do you."

Once again Hope drew strength from his support. Her resolve strengthened. She would do whatever it took to overcome this, to take these men down and restore her daughter's life to normal.

She moved away and headed into the room to where a stack of presents sat beneath a towering, fully decorated Christmas tree. "Oh, Steve." She sighed and glanced back at Ian hovering in the doorway. "Come on in and let's get started. This might take a while."

"But they're your presents."

"No time for sentimentality. We have to find whatever it is that will explain why they're after me."

She was already on her knees, tearing open the first package, but she froze and let out a soft cry as she unwrapped a book. "What did I tell you? Just look at how the cover is such a close match to this chalet." The tears that seemed ever present since she'd sent Emi off with Adam welled yet again. "Steve has been a better father figure to Emi than her father ever was." Impatiently, she swiped a hand across her face and jumped up. "Will you keep looking? I need to call Helen and check on how Steve is doing." She grabbed the phone from her pocket and smiled sadly at Ian as she hit the call button. "Dive in. Pretend you're a kid on Christmas morning. I'll just rewrap them whenever I get to give them to Emi."

By the time Hope competed her phone call and returned to Ian, he was sitting in a pile of wrapping paper with presents piled around him. A small pile of yet-to-be-opened gifts still sat beneath the tree. "Nothing yet?"

He shrugged. "Plenty of stuff to keep Emi in books and crafts for the next decade, but I don't see anything that looks remotely like a code. What's the report on Steve?"

Hope knew her face was glowing every bit as brightly as the Christmas tree as she answered. "Great news. They started bringing him out of the coma this morning. Helen says so far things are looking good. The doctors are pleased."

"Excellent news. I don't suppose he's coherent enough yet to explain all this?"

Hope shook her head. "Helen said it's a matter of layers. They do it slowly. He's still on a ventilator."

"Then back to work. Maybe we can have good news for him when he's finally fully conscious."

As Hope settled down beside him, he explained his system. "I don't know if it was intentional, but I noticed there are different wrapping papers, so I started opening the ones that were the same as Emi's book. They all seem to be for her. I left you the ones in the other paper, presuming they were personal to you."

"Thanks."

"Steve sure is generous," Ian commented as they continued to dig through the pile of presents.

"He is. He's absolutely brilliant, and he has a heart of gold. That's what confuses me so much about this. All the employees love him and he has no enemies that I know of."

"His industry is highly competitive. You never know who might be looking to take him down out of spite."

Hope shivered at the thought. "Why do people have to be so evil?"

Ian smiled gently. "No wonder my mother likes you so much. You have a gentle heart."

"I'll take that as a compliment—" Hope stopped abruptly as she noticed one more present tucked deep into the branches at the bottom of the tree. "Ian, look. The wrapping on that one doesn't match any of the others."

Every trace of fatigue fell away as Hope crawled under the tree to retrieve the present. She knew Ian's interest was piqued when he knelt beside her on the floor. Her fingers were trembling from excitement, making her fumble as she tried to unwrap the box. She flexed them and carefully undid the paper.

"Pretty amazing patience," Ian murmured. "I'd be tearing into it."

Hope glanced up at him, his face so close to hers that she felt herself sucked into the blue depths of his eyes. Suddenly she was very warm despite the chill in the house. She forced her gaze back to the package, and a thought occurred to her. "What if I'm destroying evidence by opening it?"

She sat back on her heels. "Maybe I shouldn't open it at all. What do you think?"

"It's not impossible," Ian answered slowly as he thought through the implications. "But we can't know without opening it. Steve said he sent it to you. He obviously had a reason. Just open it carefully."

Hope's fingers itched to rip the paper from the box, but she sighed deeply. He was right. Slowly she slid a finger under the tape, loosened it and eased the edges of the paper apart. She opened the box, and gently lifted the present from the box. "It's just a Christmas ornament." She sagged back, looking from the present to Ian. "I don't understand. What about a Christmas ornament could be so important that they would track me? Could we have misunderstood?"

"No." Ian picked up the ornament and rolled it around in his hand. "I think this might actually be what he meant."

Hope shook her head. "He gives Emi an ornament for the tree every year. He's been doing it since she was born. That's probably why it's wrapped differently."

"No. Look. See this seam of glue? I don't think that's original. It looks like someone forced it open and then re-sealed it. You wouldn't notice it unless you were specifically looking, and someone just seeing it hanging on the tree would never suspect anything." Ian handed her the ornament. "It's kind of ingenious, really. He sent it as a clue, but if nothing had happened to him, and he'd been able to stop the attack, you would never have even known there was something there."

"Presuming there is," Hope added.

"Only one way to find out. There should be a knife in the kitchen. Let's try to open it. I promise, if it's nothing, I'll fix it before Emi sees it."

Hope followed him into the kitchen and set the beautiful ornament on the table. It was a heavy ball shape decorated with a Currier and Ives scene labeled Christmas Past. As she studied the print, Hope mentally tipped her hat to Steve. He'd found an ornament that captured all the joy they'd been trying to create with their Twelve Days 'til Christmas platform.

She turned to Ian, who was waiting with a paring knife. "Let's do this, Doc."

Ian chuckled as he held the ornament steady with one hand and carefully slid the knife along the seam, rotating the ball as he went. When he finished, he set the knife aside and gently twisted the top and bottom in opposite directions. It split easily into two halves, and Hope gasped. Nestled inside the bottom half was a flash drive wrapped in plastic.

She threw her arms up in the air and did a little happy dance. "We did it! We found it."

Impulsively, she flung her arms around Ian and hugged him. "Thank you. Thank you for keeping at it with me." When she stepped back, she was still bubbling with happiness. "Now all we have to do is bring this to Nancy's team and see what they can figure out."

Ian stepped aside and gathered the pieces up. "We'd better get going then. It's going to be dark before long. I'll call Adam and alert him while you get ready."

Hope glanced out the window at the sky and was shocked to see how much of the day had faded away. The mountains glowed with the reflection of the setting sun, and a soft pink haze filled the pale sky as dusk settled. She wasn't eager to head to her safe house without Emi, but nothing about staying here would fill the emptiness in her heart.

Deciding it was better to leave the presents behind for now, Hope stuck the flash drive in an inside pocket of her parka and headed back to the front of the house. She pulled up short at the front door as movement outside caught her attention. "Ian," she whispered. "Please tell me I'm imagining that there are men out there by our car."

Ian came up behind her, and resting his hands on her shoulders, he peered out the window. She felt the frustration roll through his body.

"Won't lie," he muttered. "There are men out there, but now they are under our car."

"Do you think they're installing a tracking device?"

"At best."

"And at worst?" She felt his hands tense on her shoulders before he answered.

"They're planting explosives."

Hope couldn't stop the tremors that rolled through her body. "What do we do?"

"You have the flash drive?"

She nodded against his shoulder. "I just zipped it into the inside pocket of my coat."

"Okay. When I was searching before, I noticed snow-mobiles outside. Have you ever driven one?"

"A few times. I'm no expert, but I can drive in a straight line."

Ian glanced out the window again. The men were still under the car. "Let's make our escape out the back while they're busy. Make sure you're completely bundled. I'll grab some helmets."

Quietly and efficiently, they gathered their belongings and hurried to the back exit. Ian found the snowmobile keys hanging by the back door. He grabbed them and they silently headed into the yard. The house backed onto an open field of snow that spread out across the valley toward the base of the mountains.

"If we hurry, they'll have no way to follow," Ian murmured as he made sure she was properly set up on her machine and checked the fuel gauge before he settled onto his own.

Hope hit the kill switch, inserted the key into the ignition and turned it to the on position. She released the choke and waited for Ian. At his signal, they simultaneously pulled on their cords. Hope didn't know if Ian was praying, but she certainly was.

The engines revved and caught, and Hope switched to a prayer of profound gratitude.

Ian gestured for her to lead the way. Hope swallowed her fear and let the machine shoot forward. They'd only made it about a hundred yards before shouts heralded men emerging from the side of the building. She glanced over her shoulder only once, but it was enough to see rifles aimed in her direction. Remembering how the men had zigzagged several days ago to avoid Ian's shots, she did the same.

Powder kicked up beside her as the shots landed alarmingly close. "Ian," she shouted, worried that he was behind her and more of a target.

"Right here," he shouted back, his words barely audible over the whine of the snowmobiles. Riding in elaborate figure eights, Ian attempted to draw their fire away from Hope, but it seemed that only one of them had a target on their back. And that was her.

Gradually, they drew out of range, and Ian's whole body sagged in relief. He gestured to Hope, and pulled up beside her. "I think we've lost them," he called.

"I hope so," she replied. "I'd hate to be driving the whole way with them shooting at me."

He nodded. "We'll slow the pace now that we've lost them. I want to stay low and take it easy. With this new snowfall, there's the risk of avalanche if we go too high or too hard."

Hope's expression suddenly had a *Now he tells me* quality to it, and Ian had to fight back a laugh. She had to be one of the most courageous and resilient women he'd ever encountered. "Try to appreciate the beauty around you," he said with a wink.

Hope smiled and gazed at the snow-covered mountains. "God's handiwork is amazing."

*Yes, it is,* Ian thought as they moved forward, but he wasn't thinking of the mountains and sky. Appreciating Hope's beautiful heart came easily, but despite how much he tried to ignore it, he couldn't deny that her stunning physical beauty took his breath away. But that wasn't what he should be focusing on, now…or ever.

For a while they cut across the lower side of the mountain, and Ian let his tension unspool as they zipped along the tree line. The stars were starting to emerge in the deepening twilight, but the moon had yet to rise over the mountain. The still night air brought peace to his soul.

But peace didn't last long.

The unmistakable whine of approaching snowmobiles echoed across the mountains. Ian saw Hope's body go rigid. He should have known better than to let down his guard. This enemy didn't know the meaning of defeat. Every single time he thought he'd outsmarted them, they reappeared. If they weren't so dangerous, he'd admire their perseverance.

He glanced over his shoulder, but he couldn't see anyone behind them. He looked to Hope, who was pointing upward. Turning his head, Ian saw two snowmobiles steadily climbing the mountain above him, and his heart sank. If they triggered an avalanche, he and Hope would be directly in its deadly path.

The thought had barely entered his mind, when he saw one of the figures swing his arm and fling something.

Ian watched the arc of the object and rage filled him as he realized they must have hurled whatever device they'd earlier been planting on the car. He held his breath, hoping it would sputter and die. Instead, a deafening explosion echoed across the mountain as the device detonated.

Ian prayed hard, but he knew there was little chance they hadn't intentionally triggered an avalanche. Where would the snow crack, and which way would the avalanche head? As the low rumble started, and the shelf of snow started to fall away, Ian knew the answer was not in their favor. "Hope," he bellowed. "Head to the right side. As fast as you can!"

# FOURTEEN

Panic thrummed along Hope's nerves. Everywhere around her the mountain was exploding in a river of snow. *Dear Lord, help us.*

"Hope."

Ian's voice was a lifeline she could barely hear over the roar of the avalanche.

"Head to the side!" He was yelling and pointing, but all she could see was a massive wave of white cascading toward her.

"Turn hard right. Your only chance is to get to the side."

By this time, Hope wasn't even sure where the side was, but she yanked hard on her snowmobile, sending it shooting off to the right moments before the first wave of snow crashed down on them. She squeezed the accelerator as hard as she could, and the machine rode the snow as she pushed through to the edge. She turned back to ask Ian if this was far enough, but he wasn't there.

Terror poured through her. "Ian," she screamed at the top of her lungs. "Ian! Where are you? *Ian!*"

She could hear nothing over the thunderous roar of wave upon wave of snow.

Fear threatened to paralyze her, but she knew Ian's only chance at survival could very well depend on her. She had to find him. Hope pushed the snowmobile harder and raced down the slope parallel to the path of the avalanche.

Her heart caught at the sight of his snowmobile upended against a tree, but there was no sign of Ian nearby. As the snow rushed past, she braked and jumped off, forgetting she was still attached until the cord pulled loose and her engine cut off. Furiously, she dug through the snow looking for any sign Ian had been buried beneath the machine. She screamed his name until she was hoarse as she scoured the snow for a hint of his hunter green jacket or blue helmet, but all around her was nothing but an endless sea of white.

"Ian." Her voice faded to a whisper as despair overcame her. He'd been caught up in the avalanche because of her. He'd put her safety first. And he wouldn't have even been here were it not for her. Grief and guilt threatened to swamp her as surely as the snow had buried him. She couldn't give up. She owed him too much. But what could she do? Everything she'd heard about avalanches emphasized how little time you had to rescue someone, but night was falling rapidly and she couldn't even find where to look.

She fell to her knees in the snow. "Lord help me," she begged. "Give me the courage, lead me to your faithful servant, Ian."

She stood and brushed off the snow. Yes, it was dark, but the nearly full moon was rising, casting a glow over the snow-covered mountain. Determined to find Ian, she picked her way along the edge of the avalanche's path, calling his name, stopping to listen for a reply or search for any sign of him. Now that the avalanche had finished its downhill rush, an eerie silence was left behind. Over and over, she called his name into the void.

"Hope."

Her heart lifted. Was it him? She called again, but only

silence echoed back. Had he really called her name, or was she hallucinating in the cold?

"Ian," she called again and again as she trudged through the snow, conscious that with every passing moment, the chance of rescue grew slimmer.

"Hope."

The muffled voice carried on the wind, and Hope spun in circles trying to see anything in the moonlight. "Ian, where are you? I can hear you but I can't see you."

"Hope, help."

His voice was fading and panic shot through her. "Don't give up. I'm here. I'll help you."

"Over here. Quick."

Hope squinted into the shadows cast by the mountain. There, just to the left of a tree she saw an arm moving feebly. "Ian, I see you. I'm coming."

Heart pounding, she pushed through the piles of snow and rock that had come to a rest at the foot of the mountain. When she finally reached him, she fell to her knees and wanted to do nothing more than kiss him.

Shocked at her own reaction, she shook herself. The man was buried up to his neck in snow and needed serious help, not romance. Setting aside her foolishness, she started pawing at the snow around his chest. She remembered seeing a video of someone being rescued. The focus had been on first clearing the snow from his head, but then relieving the pressure around his chest so he could breathe.

"How did you survive that?" she asked. "I thought... I..." She stopped herself. He didn't need her fear or her guilt. "Can you breathe okay now?"

Ian nodded and took deep breaths of the cold, crisp air. Now that his second arm was free, he could help her loosen the snow encasing him.

"I think if you can stand and loop your arms through mine, I can use the leverage to push free."

Hope scrambled to her feet. "Like this?" she asked as she crossed behind him and fell to her knees again. She wrapped her arms under his and clasped them across his chest, then leaned back against her heels, pulling with all her might.

The first try loosened him a little, but she couldn't pull him free.

"My legs feel like they're encased in cement."

"Should I try to dig around them more?"

"No, let's just try this another time."

She resumed her position and rocked back hard on her heels. Slowly his body began to slide free.

"One more time, I think," Ian said.

Hope heard the strain in his voice. "Give yourself a moment to rest."

"Can't," he rasped. "Snow keeps filling back in."

"Okay, this is it," Hope promised. "We'll do this together. Teamwork."

She locked her arms around his chest and pulled with everything she had. Sheer determination, fueled by thoughts of the debt she owed him, gave her a superhuman strength. She pulled and pulled, feeling the resistance lessen. "Now, on three. One, two, three."

She closed her eyes to concentrate, putting everything into the final lift, and pulled.

As if being released from a giant suction cup, Ian's body slid free, but the momentum carried them over on their backs. Hope took a deep breath and opened her eyes only to find Ian's face mere inches from hers, his deep blue eyes staring gratefully down at her.

Their gazes locked, and for a long breathless moment no one said a word.

Slowly he lowered his head until his lips caressed hers, and then he kissed her with all the heightened emotion of a man who had just escaped death's grasp.

Cold wind blowing up the mountain brought Ian crashing back to reality. He pulled back, horrified that he'd let emotion overwhelm his sanity. Poor Hope must think he'd lost his mind.

"I'm so sorry," he whispered, searching for the courage to face her. But when he gazed into her eyes, he saw reflected back at him the same mix of awe and regret that he was feeling. "I don't know what came over me."

Hope smiled tremulously. "A brush with death, no doubt."

He agreed, because that made it easier on both of them, but the lingering taste of her kiss made him doubt the explanation was that easy. He pushed the thoughts away. Better that he focus on how to get out of here.

"I'm guessing my snowmobile is a loss."

Hope gulped, and he suddenly remembered hearing her screaming his name. He imagined relief that he wasn't dead might explain away her kiss too.

"It's crashed against a tree."

"Is yours still functioning?"

"I think so. I left it higher up the mountain when I was looking for you. I'll go get it."

"You don't need to go alone. I can come with you." Or did she want an excuse to get away from him?

"I'm just worried about your strength. You should rest."

He shook his head. "Not necessary. I'll probably crash later. No pun intended. But for now, I'm running on pure adrenaline."

They hiked back up the mountain, careful not to dislodge any more snow. As they passed the twisted wreckage of the snowmobile he'd been riding, Ian whispered a prayer of gratitude.

"The minute I knew I couldn't get to the side in time, I jumped off the machine. I've heard that the best thing you can do if caught in an avalanche is to try to swim with it, so that's what I did. I pretended I'd caught an ocean wave and swam as I tumbled downhill."

Hope shuddered. "I can't even imagine how terrifying it was."

He grasped her hand. "Probably pretty similar to how you felt when you saw the snowmobile and couldn't find me."

Hope hung her head a minute before she stopped and looked up straight into his eyes. "I've never been so terrified in all my life. And that includes being driven off the road, stranded in a snow cave and chased by gunmen."

"Hey," he said softly. "The snow cave was pretty cool."

Hope smiled so widely that Ian felt the warmth clear to the tips of his toes.

"You're right. It was like nothing I've ever experienced before. Now I can add surviving an avalanche to that list."

A long moment built between them as the sheer magnitude of what they'd survived crashed over them.

"Thank you," Ian murmured. "Thank you for not giving up, for finding me."

She rested a gloved hand on his cheek. "And thank you for everything you've done for Emi and for me."

He grinned. "Anytime. But before we get too carried away, let's make sure your snowmobile is still functioning."

They resumed climbing, keeping a wary eye out for any sign of their attackers, though Ian was pretty sure the avalanche had blocked them from getting down the mountain.

Hopefully, they'd seen him hit and presumed they were both dead. He shivered, thinking how very close to that reality he'd come. Hope had saved him.

When they finally reached Hope's snowmobile, Ian was relieved to see it hadn't sunk too deeply.

"Is it okay? Or do we need another snow cave?"

"It will be okay. I'm going to dig around the skis. Can you stomp down the snow ahead of us to create a firm pack? That will allow us to get free and build some momentum so we don't get stuck again, since this time it will be carrying both our weight."

"I can do that."

They got to work, and before long, Ian had the snowmobile unstuck. "Because I'm so much bigger than you, I think you should sit as far forward as you can. I'll sit behind you and reach around you to drive. I think you'll be warmer that way, but I don't want to make you uncomfortable, so let me know if you are."

"Aye, aye, Captain."

Hope climbed onto the snowmobile and hunched over the handles.

"They call that the Squirrel," Ian teased. "Because of the way you have to hold your hands."

"They can call it whatever they want," Hope replied. "As long as it gets me to the house and a warm fire."

"You still have the flash drive?"

Hope patted her coat pocket. "Safe and dry."

"Then let's head to the house." Ian climbed up on the extended seat behind her and wrapped his arms around Hope as he reached for the handles. "Ready?"

Hope nodded, and Ian set the machine in motion. He had to rock it back and forth a few times to fully break loose, but then they were off and racing back down the mountain toward the safe house and warmth.

The moon had risen, lighting their way. Snow sparkled and stars studded the dark sky. Ian allowed himself to relax and soak in the beauty of it. His head was so close to Hope's that he could whisper in her ear. "More of God's handiwork."

Even through all the layers of clothing between them, Ian felt her body sigh and relax back against his chest. They'd survived a close call with death today, but for now, with his arms wrapped protectively around her, he could just thank God that they were whole.

The night was cold, but the wind had died down, and despite everything they'd endured, it was the perfect night for a peaceful moonlit ride.

Ian decided he would cherish the peace while he could, knowing that renewed danger was as inevitable as the sunrise.

# FIFTEEN

Warm. She was finally warm.

Hope snuggled under the blanket as she rested beside the fire and fought off sleep. It would be so easy to close her eyes and just drift off.

Ian had gone outside with Nancy to wait for her team. There'd been a last-minute switch of safe houses—Adam's idea. After Ian had notified him that they'd located the drive, Adam had decided he wanted a house with a built-in cyber shield to better protect them from being hacked.

Time was running out. Hope had lost track of what day of the countdown they were on, but she knew the deadline was drawing near. They couldn't afford any errors now.

Maybe it was a good idea for her to sleep while she waited, just so she'd be sharper when they arrived. The fire was so cozy, and she'd been so cold for so long. She closed her eyes, promising herself it would be just for a little while.

Hope had no idea how much time had passed when the sound of voices roused her from a deep sleep. She blinked and yawned and was stretching under her blanket when Ian entered the room followed by a group of men and a woman she'd never seen before.

Ian came and leaned over. "Had a good sleep, I hope."

She couldn't help but smile up at him. "It was lovely. I'm just sorry you didn't have a chance to rest."

"I'm used to going long days without sleep."

"Army life?"

He nodded. "And calving season."

"I sometimes forget you're a rancher and not always my personal bodyguard," she said with a wink as she pushed back the blankets and swung her legs around. She tipped her head toward the door where the group had gathered. "What happens now?"

"Nancy will introduce you to her team, and I'll let them take it from there."

Hope stood and ran a hand through her sleep-tousled hair before following Ian across the room.

Nancy and her team stopped talking as Hope and Ian approached.

"Hope, let me introduce you to the people who are going to help us resolve this. Ned and Erin are Adam's friends, but also longtime hiking buddies of mine. They're computer whiz kids whose specialty is codebreaking. Jacob and Russ are my colleagues. They are on the cybercrime task force and have a lot of experience dealing with ransomware attacks."

Hope's heart filled at the sight of these professionals who had all gathered here to help her fight back against the ruthless men who'd hurt Steve and threatened her and Emi so many times. "I can't thank you enough. I—"

Ned cut her off with a wave of his hand and a smile. "Please, no thanks are necessary, Hope. We appreciate all the risks you've taken to get the drive for us. Nancy already filled us in on everything she knows. If we have any questions we'll let you know. Now, let's get some coffee and get to work. We've got criminals to take down."

Hope smiled her appreciation. "Nancy put the flash drive in the war room Adam created upstairs. If you want to get to work, I'll bring up the coffee as soon as it's ready. It will give me something to do other than stress."

"Sounds like a plan to me," Erin agreed.

The team trooped upstairs, and Hope got to work. Ian just stood at the counter watching. Hope could see that he was barely keeping upright, and his eyelids kept drifting closed. Once the coffee was brewing, she walked around the counter and took him by the arm. "Come on," she urged. "I happen to know where there's a really comfy sofa near a warm fire."

Ian attempted a protest, but the adrenaline crash he'd predicted took over. He was fast asleep as soon as his head hit the pillows. Hope pulled a blanket up over him and kissed his forehead. "Sleep well, my hero."

She studied him for a few minutes, puzzling over the paradox that was this man. Her hero, her protector, but also a man reluctant to let down his guard, to open up. *What secrets does that heart of yours hold, Ian?*

The coffeemaker dinged, pulling her from her thoughts before she could allow them to suck her into memories of the kiss they'd shared. A kiss she should never have allowed—or enjoyed so much.

Shoving the memory away, she focused on preparing the tray, filling it with creamer, sugar, and an array of treats she'd found in the cabinet. When all was ready, she carried it up the stairs and knocked on the door of what had been the master bedroom before Adam repurposed it.

Nancy opened the door and took the tray from her. When Hope would have turned away, Nancy beckoned her in. "Come in. I have a surprise for you."

Hope entered the room, amazed at the number of computers and the variety of different images being projected on screens. She had no idea how Adam had pulled this off so quickly, but she was learning not to underestimate the man.

Turning away from the baffling computer work, she followed Nancy to the far corner, where a smaller laptop was set up.

"I thought you might like to talk to Emi," Nancy offered. "Ned set up a secure line. As soon as you're ready, Isabelle will sign on."

Hope's hands flew to her mouth. "Seriously? It's safe?"

"You've got my thousand percent guarantee," Ned called over, his eyes never once leaving the stream of numbers and symbols that whirred across his screen.

Hope settled herself into the chair, and within minutes Emi's beloved face appeared. "Hi, Mommy. I miss you this much," she said and stretched her arms out to demonstrate. "But I'm having so much fun. Mia is my new friend, and she has a dog and her mommy is expecting a baby brother, and we did painting and coloring. Mia loves to draw pictures and she is teaching me how to draw horses so I can draw Nancy's reindeer, and tonight we're going to make a gingerbread house."

She finally had to pause for breath, and Hope jumped in. "So, you're happy there?"

"I am. Mia is the bestest friend I ever had." Her voice dipped for just a minute. "I want to come home and see you and Uncle Steve and Ian, but this is fun, so it's okay if it takes a while before you can come get me."

Hope almost laughed out loud. Here she'd been worried about Emi missing her and being miserable, and instead her daughter was having the time of her life in a place where she was safe.

"Mrs. Isabelle says I need to say goodbye because I'm going to help Mia set the table for lunch. Bye, Mommy. I love you."

Isabelle's face took the place of Emi's on the screen. "I guess you can tell for yourself that she's doing well."

"I can. Thank you so much for caring for her. That sounds like quite the energetic duo you have there."

"Oh, they're amazing together," Isabelle replied. "And we're all learning *so* many reindeer facts. Did you know that their eyes are golden in the summer, but turn deep blue in the winter?"

Hope laughed. "So I've heard."

Isabelle joined in the laughter, and her face was filled with such warmth and love that Hope found herself wrapped up in it. "I know you have to get back to them, but thank you again. I hope one day we can meet under happier circumstances."

"Count on it," Isabelle promised. "I have every confidence in my husband and his team."

The screen went dark, and Hope sat for a moment, offering a silent prayer of thanksgiving for all the generous and caring people God had sent to help her.

When she rose, she looked over at Nancy. "I think you created a monster teaching her all those reindeer facts."

Nancy laughed. "She can help out with my reindeer anytime."

Hope's mood dimmed a little at the thought of what would happen when all this was over. Would she and Emi just go back to their lonely life together? A life she'd been totally content with before.

Until she'd met Ian.

Brushing the thought aside, she turned to the team. "My

daughter just reminded me that it's lunchtime. Anyone hungry?"

Shaking heads and distracted murmurs of "no thanks" didn't really surprise her. They were all deep into the work they were doing. If only there was some way she could help.

Ian was still soundly asleep when Hope went downstairs, so she selected a book from the library shelf, poured herself a mugful of coffee and settled in a chair by the fire. With her fears for Emi dissipated, she allowed herself to relax. Her daughter wasn't the only bookworm in the family.


Ian woke, disoriented and sore. Every bone in his body ached like he'd been through the wringer. He closed his eyes and let the memories wash over him. He'd survived an avalanche. Little wonder he felt like his body had been pulverized.

With that memory came the one of what had happened in the aftermath, a kiss that had transported him out of a world of fear and pain and into one shining with possibility. Except it could never be.

He opened his eyes and could see Hope curled in a chair by the fire. She'd obviously fallen asleep while reading. The book lay abandoned on her lap and she'd nestled so that her head rested against the high back. For a moment, he indulged himself in fruitless daydreams of a life he didn't deserve.

Hope was so beautiful, inside and out. More than anything he'd ever wanted, Ian found himself yearning for a future together with her. A life with Hope and Emi would be filled with everything that was bright and loving and happy, a dream come true.

But on the wings of that dream, all his failures came rushing at him. He'd proved beyond doubt that he didn't have what it took to be a husband. Hope had already suffered at the hands of one deceitful spouse. She deserved someone so much better than him.

As if his focus had stirred her, Hope shifted slightly, opened her eyes and smiled at him.

"You're thinking again," she teased.

Ian sighed. "How do you know that?"

She yawned, stretched and straightened in the chair. "You get this serious expression. Your brows pinch together, and you look like you're sucking lemons."

"You've only known me a few days."

She laughed softly. "You've spent a lot of time thinking hard. Understandable with all we've gone through, but you really need happier thoughts."

Ian didn't respond right away, and in the silence they could hear the team members walking around up in the war room.

"You'd rather be up there with them, wouldn't you?" Hope asked.

"Hmm?"

"You'd rather be busy plotting the resolution of this mess than babysitting a morose mother who misses her little girl."

Ian smiled at her. "I miss your little girl too. I haven't learned anything new about reindeer in the past twenty hours."

Hope smiled sadly.

"Come on, that almost got a laugh," Ian teased.

"And you avoided answering."

Ian shrugged. "Once maybe, but no, not now."

"What changed that?"

"Not what. *I* changed."

"I'm sorry," Hope said softly. "I don't mean to pry. You don't have to share anything if you don't want to."

But Ian found that he did want to. "That's kind of you after we basically put your entire life under a microscope."

Hope dipped her head. "I won't deny that was hard, but it was necessary. So it's okay. I absolve you of any guilt you might be feeling about digging into my life."

Ian hesitated a moment, knowing he was about to reveal a part of himself to her that he'd never shared with another person. He wasn't completely sure he understood why he felt compelled to share it. Perhaps just a self-destructive impulse, because something about Hope was opening doors to parts of him that had been locked tight for a long time. Maybe because he needed to close them against irrational dreams that dared to try and break through.

He hung his head knowing he was about to disillusion her. He wished it was unnecessary, but he'd heard the words she whispered when she thought he was asleep. Better she realize now that he was nobody's hero before she began dreaming her own impossible dreams.

"Back at the restaurant, you asked what I was thinking." He took a long, deep breath and exhaled slowly. "I was thinking about my wife."

"You must miss her."

Her voice was soft, kind. Ian fell silent, thinking how to respond. "It's not that."

He looked over at Hope, and their eyes locked. There was a misplaced look of empathy in the way she gazed at him. Nancy had given her the wrong impression. Shelby wasn't the problem. He was the one who had failed her. Hope needed to understand why he wasn't worthy of a relationship.

"We started dating in high school. Some friends wanted a double date, so we agreed, since we knew each other from math class. We hit it off and dated for the rest of high school and college. I wasn't thinking serious or long-term, and I didn't think she was either.

"I'd decided to join the army right out of college, following in my dad's footsteps. Shelby wasn't very happy about that. But I wouldn't change my mind.

"That's when she started to push about getting married before I left." He paused. "I don't want you thinking I'm saying that to make her sound bad. It was a thing with her group of friends at the time. They all wanted to get married before they graduated. I guess I got caught up in the idea of it too—the knowledge that someone would be waiting for me to come home."

He took a deep breath and exhaled. "That was really selfish of me. Shelby wanted more. She needed someone to come home to, also. And I wasn't there. The more time I served, the more committed I became. War does things to you. It messes with your head. Even when I was home on leave, I wasn't the husband she needed."

Hope was sitting quietly, listening. There was no judgment on her face, but he knew that would change.

"She was desperate to have a baby. For years, I believed she thought that if we had a family, I'd resign and come home." He shrugged. "Maybe I would have. I was excited when she got pregnant. But then she miscarried. For a time, we were closer. I was home for a bit. But then, just after she found out she was pregnant again, I was called up. I was deployed when she lost that baby. There were two more miscarriages, and I begged her to give up. We could adopt. We could just be the two of us. But she wanted to try again."

Ian's voice was cracking, and he stayed silent until he could speak without emotion dragging him down. "I was gone again, by the time she found out she was pregnant.

We'd had harsh words before I left. She begged me to stay, said she needed me."

"But you were in the army. You didn't have a choice."

He shrugged. "That's true. But what haunts me is that I wanted to go. I was more at home with my squad by then than I was with Shelby. I knew that it made me a terrible husband."

He let out a heavy sigh. "In hindsight, and with help, I came to understand that it was one of the effects of war. My thinking had become skewed by the life I was living. But that didn't help Shelby." He buried his head in his hands.

Hope rose from her chair and came to sit on the floor in front of Ian. She felt the pain pouring out of him and needed to be close, to offer comfort the way he had comforted her. She pulled his hands from his face and held them tightly. "What happened?"

"There were complications. She died and so did my son."

"Oh, Ian." Whatever she had been expecting it was not this.

"I was so angry."

The look in his eyes when he raised them to meet hers broke her heart. "Of course you were. That was a horrible thing to have happen."

He looked down at her, and the agony was raw on his face. "No." He shook his head. "I was angry at her." His voice fell to a whisper. "At myself."

Hope went still. This was it. She understood that what he was holding inside himself over this was the dark pain she glimpsed every so often when he thought no one was looking.

"I found out that the doctor had told her not to get pregnant again. He told her it could cost her life and her baby's." He swallowed hard before continuing. "She risked it anyway. Because she wanted to be a mother more than anything in the world." He had to pause for another deep breath. "I think I knew on some level that she risked it because she needed a child, she needed someone to need her in a way I didn't, couldn't. She needed someone to be there with her. And I wasn't."

"Ian—" Hope tried to protest, but he started talking again, his voice hoarse.

"When you started talking in the restaurant about how it felt to have to let Emi go, something broke loose in my brain, and I finally understood. Shelby had been sacrificing so much. Each time she lost a child, she lost a bit of herself. And I was too caught up in my own life to realize it. All these years I've been angry at her for the choice she made going against the doctor's advice. I thought she was trying to manipulate me, knowing we were drifting apart. But it wasn't that at all. I failed her. And I can never make it up."

Hope didn't even know what to say. She could only hold on to his hands and pray for the words. She didn't have the power to heal him. Only God could do that.

"Have you prayed about this?"

Ian seemed startled by her question. "What would I have prayed for? It was too late to bring her back."

"For healing. For you to learn to forgive—Shelby and yourself."

Ian stood, and Hope felt the connection between them breaking. "I've prayed for her and for our little boy." His voice cracked. "I've prayed to God to take away my anger at her." He gave a harsh laugh. "I guess He heard that prayer. All this time, the one I should have been angry with was myself."

Grief formed a lump in Hope's chest. She could barely

speak. "If that was the lesson you took away from what I said today, then I'm sorry, but you misunderstood." She stood and faced him. "I know a little bit about what it's like to be in Shelby's shoes. My husband didn't want me in his life either."

Ian looked up, startled. "No. I didn't mean it like that. I never cheated on her."

He hung his head and kept talking. "I'm sorry. I didn't mean to remind you. You asked what I was thinking earlier. I shared this because I wanted you to know that your courage today affected me deeply. It made me see things differently. You changed my feelings about what happened."

Hope waited, sensing that he wasn't done. "I'll still carry the anger and guilt, but those feelings won't be directed at her."

"Is that why Nancy doesn't like her? Because you blame yourself?"

"What?"

"I've heard Nancy compare me to Shelby a couple of times." She rolled her eyes. "It was never a compliment to Shelby."

Ian shook his head. "You're right. Nancy wasn't a fan of Shelby, but it's not because of me, even though she never wanted me to marry her. They were best friends once, then something happened. I don't know what it was, but they were rivals after that. All through high school."

Before Hope could reply, a resounding "Yes!" echoed from upstairs. Hope looked at Ian.

"Let's go," he said, and they ran for the stairs.

# SIXTEEN

Nancy was high-fiving her team as Hope and Ian burst through the door. "We did it!" she exclaimed. "Steve's drive held enough samples of code that we were able to match the fingerprint to a known hacker."

Hope blinked in confusion. "They left a fingerprint on the drive?"

Ned answered. "Yes and no. Not a fingerprint in the literal sense that we could test for a match, though that would have been nice too. This is more specific to coding. The best way I can think of to explain it is if you asked two people to write about the same thing. Supposing they were sufficiently literate, you'd still get two very different texts. It's the sentence syntax, the word choice. That sort of thing. The stylistic expression. Coding is a little like that. The basic code is the same, but the way each person puts it together reflects their style. Steve got us started. He'd gathered samples to point us in the right direction. I'm guessing he wasn't far from cracking it when he was attacked."

"So that might explain the attack at the office?" Ian prompted. "If the person suspected it. But how would they know?"

As Ned spoke, and Hope recalled Ian's comments about Nancy and Shelby being rivals, something clicked in her brain. "I think Steve knew who it was and was just trying to prove it," she replied.

"What do you mean?" Jacob asked as he swung around to face her. "This person isn't widely known. He's the leader of a cyber gang that has been sabotaging small-town banks and mom-and-pop companies. The gang has flown under the radar because they haven't been going for the major corporations or governments that would draw national media and law enforcement attention."

Hope spoke up. "*She* was honing her craft."

"What?"

"I know who is behind this."

All eyes were on her now, so Hope began to explain.

"Ian said something to me a few minutes ago. It triggered a connection. Back in college, Steve had another partner besides my deceased husband—a woman he was dating. My roommate for the beginning of sophomore year. She had transferred in and was given a suite with me. She and Steve met the first weekend and hit it off instantly. She was more than a computer geek. She was brilliant, probably the smartest person I've ever known." Hope paused, fighting back a swell of emotion.

"There were rumors of a scandal at her last school, but she seemed really nice and the four of us were a thing for a while. She and Steve had a class together, and they were working on some supersecret project. He caught her cheating. I don't know all the details because I didn't understand any of it at the time—something about accessing other people's files. She got kicked out of school. Steve was heartbroken. He told me later that he'd been the one to turn her in.

"He got over her, and we all moved on. I haven't thought of her in a decade or more. But when Ian and I were talking before, something reminded me of her... Adrianna. This, more than arrogance, explains why Steve was trying to undo what she'd done. I'm sure he realized right away who it was. I imagine it was a personal challenge to him to defeat her. To let good win."

She fell silent, then added quietly, "It probably also explains why she's been coming after me. She would know that the way to hurt Steve was through me. She was jealous of our friendship."

"Why now though?" Erin asked.

Hope shrugged. "I can't say for sure, but I'd guess because of the success of Twelve Days 'til Christmas. And the fact that it was something Steve and I did together."

She could see doubt lingering on a few faces. "If you have a secure line, I could call the hospital. They were bringing Steve out of his coma yesterday. Maybe he's alert by now and can confirm."

Ned handed her a phone, and Hope immediately dialed Helen's number. Her nerves were thrumming as she waited for Steve to confirm what she knew in her heart. The phone rang through to voicemail, so she tried again. *Pick up. Pick up.*

"Hello?" Helen's hesitant voice came over the line.

"Helen, it's Hope. Is Steve awake yet? Can he talk?"

"Hope, where are you? Is everything okay?"

"I'll explain the ins and outs later. I just need to know if he can talk."

Helen's voice was heavy. "He's still on a respirator. It's been a slow process. He can't talk."

Hope's heart sank, but she wasn't giving up. "Does he respond at all?"

"He squeezed my hand." Helen's voice lightened with those words, and Hope could almost feel her smile.

"I have something really important I need you to do. Talk to him. Tell him I'm on the phone."

Hope listened while Helen spoke gently.

"His eyes opened!"

Hope let out a huge sigh. "Ask him this. Is it Adrianna?"

"What?"

"He'll know what it means. Watch carefully for his re-action."

Hope waited. So much would hinge on Steve's response.

"Hope? His eyes grew wide and he squeezed my hand. He tried to nod."

Chills raced along Hope's arm and radiated out through her body. She closed her eyes and drew a breath. "Thank you. Tell him…" Her voice broke. "Tell him I'll take care of it. I have a team. He just needs to concentrate on getting well so he can see Emi for Christmas and give her the re-paired ornament himself." She listened while Helen repeated her message verbatim.

"He smiled, Hope. He smiled."

Tears flooded Hope's eyes as she said her goodbyes and handed the phone back to Ned.

"Take a minute," he said gently. "We've got this now. We'll take her down."

Hope sniffed and nodded. When she turned around, Ian was smiling softly at her.

"Come on." He rested an arm around her shoulder and led her from the room. "I think they're going to be busy for a while. Let's go cook dinner."

All of the tension from their earlier conversation van-ished as they opened cabinets, scoured the fridge and tried to settle on a meal plan. "Adam really thought of every-thing, didn't he?" Hope commented as she peered into the freezer compartment. "Although the amount of food is a little disconcerting. Does he really expect it to take so long to fix this?"

Ian laughed. "Nope, that's just Adam. Prepared for any emergency."

"Well, I, for one, am very grateful. Problem is Emi's tastes run to finger foods and pizza." Her voice dropped. "It's been a long while since I fed a group. I don't even know what to do with any of this."

"No worries. I've got it."

"What, you're a soldier, a rancher, a Christmas tree guy and…a chef?"

Ian whipped a towel over his shoulder and picked up a knife. "Prepare to be dazzled."

Hope burst out laughing. "I prefer to be fed."

"All in good time, my dear. Alas, I find myself in need of a sous-chef. Are you available?"

"Ah, he speaks French as well. *Mais oui, monsieur.*"

Ian laid out an array of vegetables and handed her a paring knife. "If you'll peel these, I'll tend to the roast."

Hope set happily to work feeling more content than she had in a long while. Yes, they were still under threat, but she had confidence in the team Adam had assembled. Her daughter was safe and happy, and she was in a cozy kitchen cooking with a man…with a man who, if she were being honest, she wished could be part of her future.

But even if she could have gotten past the fear and doubt in her own heart, their conversation earlier made it clear Ian was still buried in the guilt and grief of his past. She'd barely survived marriage with a man who didn't love her enough. She owed it to both her daughter and herself to never settle for that again.

Ian loaded the last of the dishes into the dishwasher and picked up a cloth to wipe down the counter while Hope poured tea. The evening stretched ahead of them, and he needed a way to fill it that would keep him from wanting to kiss her. He'd been fighting the memories of their impulsive kiss on the mountain slope all day, but they were never going to fade as long as she was with him, smiling, teasing and chatting happily.

He'd developed a deep admiration watching the way she coped with adversity, forging ahead no matter what obstacles appeared. And seeing her with his family, blending in, befriending his mother and sister—it was like the universe had designed an entirely new way to torment him. But this cozy domesticity elevated the torture to a whole new level. This was all he had ever wanted of life: someone who could be a partner, a friend, a—

"Ian, you're going to rub the finish right off that counter." Hope rested her hand over his. "What is it? What's bothering you?"

He looked down into her eyes and saw the same glimmer he knew must be reflected in his own. A wish for something that couldn't be.

Pulling away, he tossed the rag in the sink. "Just impatient, I guess. Wondering how long it will take them to execute their plan."

Hope picked up her tea mug. "I saw a chess set in the library. Do you play?"

"I do actually."

"Good. Then you can teach me," she called as she headed out of the kitchen. She stopped in the doorway and grinned back at him. "Fair warning, I've never been able to get the hang of it."

Ian shook his head and followed behind her. "That's what Nancy's husband said just before he whomped me."

Hope stopped short. "Nancy is married?"

Ian glanced up the staircase before following Hope into

the library. He lowered his voice. "She was. Her husband was killed in combat a little over a year ago."

Tears sprung to Hope's eyes. "That makes me feel even worse for involving her in this."

"Don't," Ian reassured her. "Working, keeping her mind occupied, it's how she has dealt with her grief. She'd let you know if she couldn't handle it." Even as he said the words, Ian wondered if they were really true. He had a nagging feeling that Nancy hadn't dealt with her loss any better than he had his. Both had submerged their grief in work.

Which was what he needed to do now. Focus on Hope and the job they had to do. He settled himself in front of the chessboard and grinned at her. "Ready?"

An hour later, the chessboard lay abandoned and Hope was curled on the sofa. "I told you. I just don't have a head for it." She laughed. "I think I've spent too many hours playing board games with Emi."

"How's she doing with all this? Nancy said you spoke to her earlier."

"I did." She shook her head in bemusement. "She's having the time of her life and says Mia is her 'bestest' friend. My shy little girl is making friends all over the place. Isabelle may have a bone to pick with Nancy though. Apparently they're being inundated with reindeer trivia."

Ian threw back his head, laughing. "She's quite the little charmer." *Just like her mother.*

Hope stretched and propped a pillow beneath her head. "So how do you know Adam and Isabelle?"

"Adam and I are both veterans. We met in a local wilderness therapy group."

"That sounds intriguing. Tell me more."

Ian stared into the blazing fire for a long moment before answering. "I told you that war does something to you," he said abstractedly. "It's not like you think when you sign up—all guns and glory." He buried his face and massaged his brow. "You see a lot of things you'll never be able to unsee, get called to take risks that strike fear in your heart. But you do it all anyway because you know your country is counting on you."

He looked up and saw that Hope was sitting up, fully concentrating on him and what he was saying.

"You're on, 24/7. So, when you come home…it can be hard to adjust, find a purpose." He stood, uncomfortable with expressing his thoughts, needing to move. "It wasn't as bad for me as for some. Adam had a tough time of it." He looked over at her and smiled. "He's doing great now though. Wilderness therapy taught us to reconnect with ourselves through nature. Then he met Isabelle and Mia." He hesitated, thinking of how much Adam's situation had been like his own. He met Isabelle when she was also being pursued by men with an intent to kill. Ian swallowed hard before continuing. "Making a family with them has been the best thing ever for him."

"That veterans' center in town, the one the Christmas trees were for, that's important to you, right?"

Ian glanced at her and saw the wheels churning in her head. "Very."

She jumped up and started pacing. Her face was twisted in the cutest expression, and Ian couldn't decide if he should be excited or wary of what was causing it.

"Who's going to wear a hole in the rug?"

The question jolted Hope from her thoughts. "What? Oh!" She started to laugh. "Sorry, I get excited when the ideas start popping."

"I can see that. Want to share?"

She bit her lip. "I've been wracking my brain trying to

think of some way to repay you for what you've done for Emi and me."

"There's no need—"

She put a finger over her lips to shush him. "Not for you, maybe. But it's something I need to do. And I think I have an idea how." She cast a glance at the discarded chess pieces. "I may not be much good at chess, but there is one thing I'm really good at, and that's not me being boastful."

Ian looked away, unable to bear the beauty shining forth from her spirit. "And what would that be?" he asked hoarsely.

"I'm really good at marketing things, at creating campaigns to raise awareness." She walked toward where he was standing by the fireplace and lifted his hands in hers. "I'd like to repay you by helping raise awareness—and money, of course—for your veterans' center, for the wilderness therapy. Not just at Christmas, but all year long, to help people like you and Adam, who give so very much to help others."

She gazed up at him, waiting for his answer.

There really was only one answer he could give. With the firelight glinting off her blond hair, and her eyes gleaming with such generosity and kindness, Ian gave in to what he'd been fighting so helplessly and he kissed her again.

# SEVENTEEN

Believing in Ian, wanting to help him…and losing herself in his kiss…were very different things. The part of Hope that had been lonely for so long, the brave version of herself who was trying to build a new life, that part wanted her to surrender, to allow her brain to accept what her heart knew. She was falling in love with this incredible man.

But her brain knew what her heart failed to recognize, that this man was wounded in a way she couldn't heal, that he had too many issues he needed to resolve, and she couldn't risk her daughter's happiness on a fragile hope that he could come to love her too.

But she couldn't bear to hurt him. Not after all he'd done for her.

Slowly, she drew back, resting her hand on his cheek and gazing into his eyes—eyes that flared with conflicted feelings that told her she was right.

She closed her eyes a moment to compose herself, then drew a breath and spoke. "I care for you, Ian. More than I should. And I'm so very grateful for everything you've done for me, for my daughter."

She lowered her gaze, knowing she couldn't hide what burned in her heart, what must be reflected in her eyes, and forced out the words she didn't want to say. "This is wrong.

We can't mistake gratitude for something more, can't make promises we won't keep. Can't pretend we could share a…"

Her voice broke before she could add the word *future*, and she turned and rushed from the room. Humiliation flooded her. In trying to be kind, she'd said much more than she'd intended. In telling him what they couldn't have, she'd revealed what she yearned for.

Needing to focus on what she *was* here for, Hope hurried up to the war room, hoping she'd find they'd made some progress, that this could all be over soon, and she and Emi could go home.

Hope fixed a smile on her face when Nancy answered her knock at the door. "Any luck up here with the genius squad?" she asked, her voice deliberately light.

Nancy ushered Hope back into the hallway and pulled the door closed behind her. "Don't want to risk disturbing them. They're making some progress, but it's slow work, because you have to do it without alerting the enemy."

Hope shivered. Nancy's language put the name of the room in perspective and reminded her there was much more at stake than her aching heart. They were fighting a war against evil behind those doors. "What exactly are they trying to do?"

"It's a complicated process. First they have to reverse hack and steal back the data she took from all the people who play on your platform. Then we take her site down, and finally, once she's powerless, we close the trapdoor in Twelve Days 'til Christmas so it's completely safe."

Hope's emotions boomeranged between awe and a sense of futility. She wanted to be in the room watching, helping, but Steve had been right. She understood nothing about this part. Her expertise had been in making everyone want to be part of their cyber family. "I feel so useless. All of you are going to these lengths to resolve my problem, while I sit here twiddling my thumbs."

"Don't underestimate your contribution, Hope," Nancy said gently. "You made a valuable connection. *You* told us about Adrianna. And don't worry about them. They're taking down a hacker who could grow into someone who someday could pose a risk to national security. It's what they do all day, every day—just not always with a ticking clock and such urgency."

This *was* like a ticking clock, and Hope suddenly realized she had no idea how close to the deadline they actually were. "I've completely lost track of time."

"Six days 'til Christmas."

Hope sighed sadly. "It's Christmas-movie day. Emi and I were supposed to watch *Miracle on 34th Street* tonight."

Nancy laid a hand on Hope's arm. "When this is over—and it will be—you and Emi can have a lifetime of watching movies together."

Hope caught herself. "You're right. I'm sorry." She sighed again. "I think it's all just catching up with me because I have nothing to do."

"That brother of mine isn't entertaining you?"

Hope's blush gave her away and Nancy smirked.

"Oh, no," Hope assured her. "It's not like that."

"Too bad," Nancy answered. "He needs someone like you. No, scratch that," she said as she opened the war room door. "He doesn't need someone like you—he needs you. Think about it," she said as she shut the door.

For the next two days, Hope couldn't think of anything else.

She knew Nancy was wrong. She and Ian had too many unhealed wounds to be able to make anything work between them. But still the thoughts tantalized. *What if?*

So, she prayed and made food, and brought coffee when needed, caught some sleep when she could, and two days passed at a snail's pace while she tried her best to avoid Ian. The ease, the bond they'd shared, had been severed with a kiss. He was too mired in the past, and she was too scared to be hurt again.

But she missed him.

Ian thought he was losing his mind. How could you miss someone so badly when you'd known them less than a week and were living in the same house?

But time and distance were both relative, and though he and Hope were technically living within the same square footage, he'd barely seen her, even in passing, since his ill-timed kiss.

He busied himself chopping wood for the fireplace, read the books he didn't usually have time for, poked his head into the war room to see if he could help and he stewed wondering how he'd managed to mess things up so badly that they couldn't even be friends.

But truth was, he didn't want Hope for friendship alone. He wanted her for a lifetime, if only he was worthy. She deserved so much more than a man who carried a burden of guilt.

"Ian, Hope! Come in here. We did it!"

Ian didn't think he'd ever heard Nancy sound so euphoric. He went running up the stairs only to collide with Hope on the landing. She smiled shyly, and his heart cracked. He smiled back, and pushed aside the tension of the past two days. "Let's go see what they've done."

The mood in the war room could only be described as cautiously victorious. Ned had fireworks exploding on his monitor. Erin was on the phone speaking quietly but smiling broadly. Jacob and Russ were standing by a screen, their bodies more relaxed than he'd seen them in days. The tension had eased for the team too.

As Hope and Ian entered, Erin disconnected her call and Ned came forward to speak with them. "It's done. We've taken back all the data, and her server is destroyed." He grinned. "Christmas is saved!"

Hope was beaming. "Have you told Steve yet?"

"No. He's been helping us a little, answering questions via Helen, but he still can't fully communicate. We thought you should be the one to tell him."

"What about Adrianna?" Ian hated to spoil their fun, but he couldn't forget that their problems in the past week had been in the real world, not just their virtual community. "What's to keep her from going after Steve or Hope as revenge?"

"We've had a team back at headquarters monitoring her since we began the final takedown," Nancy answered. "My boss was worried she might try to leave the country, so we have surveillance in place. They just notified me that she's on the move. We have eyes in the sky and cars tailing her. They're playing hopscotch so as not to tip her off."

"Can you share a screen so we can see?" Ian pushed.

"Let me see." Nancy picked up her phone and relayed the request back to her home office. She waited for a reply, then opened the link that came through. The front monitor flickered, and the scene came to life.

"What are we supposed to be seeing?" Hope asked as she walked up beside Nancy.

"See that red sports car? It's the fifth car in the right lane."

Hope groaned. "Of course. That's Adrianna. Always had to have the flashiest of everything."

"We have several aircraft in the air monitoring her car so she doesn't pick up on the tail."

"Oh, she'll pick up on it," Hope muttered.

"You don't trust us?"

"I know her. She's wily."

For a time, Hope stood, her eyes glued to the screen, but as time wore on, and Adrianna continued her drive, stopping for coffee, stopping at a fast-food restaurant, then a nail salon, Hope grew restless. "Is it safe to check into the platform now that you've taken down her server? No one has been monitoring the community for days now."

Ned glanced over his shoulder. "Yes. There's a computer on the far desk that we've been using to check in on it. You can use that."

Hope grabbed a mug of lukewarm coffee off the table and headed toward the desk. She shouldn't complain about this state of limbo compared to the danger they'd been in, but she was so ready for this to all be over. She glanced across the room at Ian, who looked up and then quickly away. She needed to be away from him, so her heart could begin to put itself back together again.

Forcing her attention away from Ian, she settled at the computer and logged into her account on the platform. Immediately photos started to load, a kaleidoscope of images that had been accumulating in the days she'd been offline. She relaxed back in the chair and allowed a feeling of satisfaction to settle over her. All of these people, her community, had been partying on, unaware of the threat that hung over them. It was a sober reminder of how fragile security on the web really was. But they were safe now. Their data was secure. The mastermind behind it had been defeated, if not captured yet. Glancing over at the men and women she had come to know and respect, Hope felt a profound sense of gratitude that there were people like them whose entire lives were dedicated to keeping the innocent safe.

But as she scrolled through her virtual community, she couldn't shake the feeling that it had been tainted. The sparkling trees and merrily lit homes had lost their luster. In her heart she knew it wasn't entirely due to Adrianna and her evil scheme. It was that she'd had a taste of the real thing, the sense of family and home that she'd come to love with Ian's family. And she wanted more of that.

But her community was for people, like herself, who didn't have that in their lives. She shouldn't dismiss the good her platform had done just because it was a pale facsimile of the real thing.

She scrolled through more photos, and gradually her heart began to lighten. These people were having fun. They might not all be with real family and friends, but that had been the point in designing this—to create a safe space where people could come together even when far apart and find a version of family and community to fill the gaps in their lives.

The murmuring voices across the room grew more animated, so Hope glanced up at the screen. Adrianna's car was alone on the road now, speeding along some mountain highway. Snow was starting to fall, and Hope shivered. There was part of her that never wanted to see snow again. She turned back to the screen, clicked on her profile page and waited for her photo stream to load. It had been a while since she'd posted anything. And it would be a while longer before she felt comfortable. Even knowing the site was secure, she was hesitant...

Her breath caught in her throat as her eyes took in the photo on the screen. Emi, with another little girl that could only be Mia, was stretched out on the white ground mak-

ing snow angels. And parked, so that just the side was visible, was a red sports car.

The message cloud was flickering, so with trembling
fingers she clicked it and a greeting appeared.

You didn't really think you'd gotten off that easily did
you, Hope?

Your people may have taken down my server, but I
have your daughter.

Who's the one who really pays the highest price?
Merry Christmas xoxo

Hope screamed, and the mug fell from her hands, shat-
tering on the floor.

# EIGHTEEN

Ian was the first to reach Hope. "What is it?"

She was trembling uncontrollably and couldn't get the words out, so she just pointed at the screen.

Ian glanced at the monitor and his heart sank. "Nancy, Ned, you need to come look at this."

Nancy started across, but Ned's shout drew all their attention back. Ian and Hope looked across at the big screen just in time to see the red car shoot off the mountain road and over the cliff before exploding into a massive fireball.

Hope gave a soft whimper and fainted dead away. Ian leaped and caught her just before she hit the ground.

The room around them was a cacophony of voices, ringing phones and frantic replays, but Ian's attention was solely on Hope. He couldn't begin to consider his own grief at the moment as he thought of what Hope must have been feeling in that moment before she lost consciousness.

He carried her across the room and laid her on the sofa, then knelt beside her to check her pulse. Her eyes flickered, but he didn't have the heart to try to wake her. She would have to face this soon enough.

Nancy rushed over to his side. "What happened? Why did she faint?"

Ian swallowed hard. "Emi." He couldn't bring himself to say the words. "Go look at the computer she was using."

She dashed across the room, and Ian knew from her muffled gasp the minute she put it together. She grabbed her phone and ran out of the room.

Ian sat on the floor beside Hope. He'd never felt so hopeless, so useless. What did you say to the woman you loved who had just watched her child die in a fiery explosion? He remembered Hope asking if he'd prayed about Shelby, so now he bowed his head and prayed with all his heart— for Hope, for Emi and, even though he struggled with it, for forgiveness for Adrianna, who had caused all this pain.

Hope's soft whimpers yanked him from his prayers and he turned to see her curling in on herself. He rose and sat beside her on the sofa, pulling her into his arms, trying to absorb her anguish. She clung to him as the whimpers turned to sobs, and he held her close as she drenched his sweater with her tears. He rocked her gently, the way he imagined she had once rocked Emi, and tears sprung to his own eyes. His heart was broken, so he couldn't even fathom the depth of her grief.

Ian didn't know how much time had passed while they sat like that before Nancy burst through the door, her face wreathed in smiles.

"Hope, it's okay. Look at me. It's okay. Emi is fine. She wasn't in the car."

Ian felt the waves of emotion roll through Hope's body as she pulled away from him. She stared at Nancy through swollen eyes, but as the words penetrated, joy danced across her face.

"You wouldn't lie to me, Nancy?"

"No, I promise. Look! I reached Isabelle. She assured me no one took that photo today and the girls are fine."

She paused. "I figured you wouldn't want Emi to see you so upset, so she sent me this video instead."

Hope pushed herself up on her elbows. Ian moved aside to make room for her as she swung her legs around and sat upright, but she linked his arm and held him close as Nancy put the phone in her other hand.

Emi's face filled the screen, laughing as she waved and called, "Hi, Mommy. This is Mia. We've been baking cookies all morning with Mrs. Isabelle. I made a special one for you."

Emi held up a red heart with a Santa hat, and Hope choked back a sob. With disbelieving eyes, she looked up at Nancy. "You're sure? You're absolutely sure?"

The smile Nancy gave in return lit her entire face. "As sure as I am that Emi loves reindeer."

Hope turned in Ian's arms, looked up at him and burst into tears all over again. "She's alive. My baby girl is alive."

Ian felt his own tears spilling over as he held her close. He raised his eyes and whispered, "Thank you, Lord."

He was grateful that Nancy left them alone, even if she did wink at him as she sauntered away. He had so many questions, and he knew Hope would too once her mind calmed, but for now, he just held her and let relief wash over them both.

Hope had never felt such joy in all her life. But as she finally lessened her grip on Ian, and slowly weaned herself from his embrace, questions began to flood her mind. "I need some answers," she told him.

Ian smiled gently at her as she eased away. "I figured you might. Should we go ask them?" He angled his head to the front of the room where Nancy and Ned were watching the video replay yet again, and Jacob and Russ were manning the computers. Erin was back on the phone.

Hope stood and started across the room, shaky at first, but she grew steadier with each step. Nancy turned and smiled at her. "You have questions, I presume."

"I need answers," she repeated.

"I have analysts looking at the photo. It's fake, no question. They're trying to trace how and when she posted it, but it's going to take a little time since she was using a new device which presumably was incinerated in the crash."

"She was in the car?"

"Adrianna? Yes."

"So…" Hope wasn't quite sure how to ask this. "Was it a deliberate crash?"

"We have a reconstruction team on the way to the accident site. Local authorities have it cordoned off, but our guys will figure out what happened."

Erin joined them. "When she came out of that last tunnel, she was traveling at a high rate of speed. It's possible she lost control. The weather conditions would have made the road slick."

Hope nodded solemnly. "What about the men who were working for her? The ones who tried to kidnap me?"

Erin had the answer to that, too. "They've been rounded up. Once we had Adrianna's name and the image of the tattoo you described to the sheriff, it wasn't hard to find her henchmen. They're no longer a threat to you."

"Then I have just one more question. Can I go home now? I need to see my daughter."

Nancy smiled at Ned. "You want to answer that?"

"Adam will be delivering Emi to the chalet at Christmas Village this afternoon. If you and Ian leave now, and go by car this time—" he grinned "—you'll beat them there by a few hours."

Hope lowered her face into her shaking hands. She couldn't believe this whole sorry story was finally over. "What about the Twelve Days finale?"

He shrugged. "That's up to you. I'm sure no one would blame you if you wanted to call it off."

"No." Hope straightened and spoke with resolve. "That would be handing Adrianna a posthumous victory. I may have to change the location and even what we're doing, but I'll talk to Steve. We will figure something out."

"You could live stream it from the ranch, right Nancy?"

Nancy looked startled at Ian's suggestion, but quickly agreed. "Sure. Mom would be in her glory. We could set up out by the reindeer barn if that works for you."

"Thank you," Hope replied warmly. "I'll check with Steve." She looked at Ian. "And your mom. But for now, I just want to get going. If you're really coming with me, we have some presents to rewrap."

He winked. "What are you waiting for?"

"A car?"

Nancy laughed. "You can take my truck. I'll hitch a ride back with Ned."

Hope turned to the other team members and found herself suddenly choked up. "I don't even know where to begin, how to thank you. You've saved my daughter's life and mine, and you saved millions of people from an identity risk they never even knew about. Words fail me."

Russ spoke up. "No thanks necessary. I'd say that it's just part of the job, but I know I speak for all of us that this was more than just the job. We were truly happy to help, Hope. Just give Emi a hug from all of us."

Hope worked her way around the circle of team members hugging each in turn. "You know that fable about the lion and the mouse? Well, I feel like the tiny mouse and you are all undoubtedly lions in your work. It feels silly to say, but if there is ever anything I can do for any of you, just say the word."

She turned to Ian. "I'm ready."

They headed to the door, and Hope found herself overcome with emotion. In these past few days this team had become like family to her. "I love you all. Thank you again."

And then she hurried down the stairs before she burst into tears again.

Hope was quiet as Ian drove toward the highway. If it was this hard to say goodbye to a team she'd known for three days, how was she ever going to bear saying goodbye to Ian?

"Penny for your thoughts?" His voice broke through her reverie, but she wasn't about to share what she'd been thinking.

"As I recall that didn't work too well with you," Hope responded softly.

They both fell silent then, remembering how it had gone when he did share his deepest thoughts. Hope wished she could find the words to break through to him, but as much as she had clung to him, relied on him, cried all over him, nothing had really changed. He was still hung up in his past, needing to make amends for something he hadn't been able to control.

# NINETEEN

Even in daylight, Christmas Village sparkled, and Hope's heart brightened with pleasure that Emi would finally be able to revel in it. The expectation of her daughter's joy eased the pang in her own heart that had only grown deeper with each mile that passed. The ride had been unbearably awkward. Neither of them was able to speak of the tenderness Ian had shown her or the way she'd sobbed out her heartbreak in his arms. It was as if they mutually understood it had been an extraordinary situation that had no bearing on their inability to make their way past their individual pain. A relationship begun on such rocky ground held no promise, yet her heart ached, wishing for what she couldn't have.

She'd spent most of the drive staring out the window at the passing scenery, reliving each moment of the past week in her mind. A gentle snow had begun to fall, but the flakes were soft and fluffy and posed no threat. Maybe in time she'd be able to enjoy snow without the fear of freezing to death.

Ian cleared his throat as he pulled into the driveway of the chalet. The FBI had removed his vehicle and taken it in so forensics could do their work. He shut off the ignition and turned to Hope. "I know you were kidding back there about needing my help to wrap presents, and I do need to get back to the ranch, but if you want me to come in and help you get set up…"

His voice trailed off as she shook her head.

Much as it pained her, a clean break would be better. "I think I need some time alone to get my head together before Adam arrives with Emi."

He nodded. "Whatever you think is best. Let me know about setting up the live stream if you decide to do it."

Hope thought her heart might crack wide open if she sat there another moment. "I will. I'll talk to Steve about it." She opened the truck door, but before she stepped out, she turned back to him. "If I couldn't find the words to thank Nancy and her team, I don't know where I'll ever find the words to thank you." She managed a smile. "But I did work up a proposal to promote your veterans' center. I'll see that you get it. Thank you."

*And goodbye.*

Hope didn't say the last two words aloud, but she knew he heard them anyway.

She hopped down from the truck and ran for the front door without looking back, because she knew if she did, she wouldn't be able to stop herself from running and begging him to stay.

She opened the door to the chalet and was slapped with memories of being here with Ian. Images of him seated under the tree, tearing open the wrapping paper flashed through her mind.

He'd been on this journey with her every step of the way from the moment she'd hidden in his truck. She wouldn't have survived without him.

Guilt swamped her. She shouldn't have sent him away so abruptly. But what else could she have done? With her hand still on the doorknob, she recalled standing there with him and seeing the men installing explosives under the truck. He'd saved her from death then, just like he had so many times. She owed him her life.

Why couldn't she risk her heart?

Should she call him back?

Sadly, she pushed the door closed. No. He'd shown all too clearly that he was still wedded to his wife in memory if not in life.

Acknowledging that it was time for a new chapter in her life, Hope turned and walked into the room. She had a lot to do to ready the house for her daughter. The daughter who was alive despite her worst fears. Tucking her sadness about Ian into a corner of her heart, she shed her coat, deliberately leaving her phone in her pocket so she wouldn't be tempted to call him, and set to work rebuilding Christmas. Thanks to Steve, there was a veritable mountain of presents to rewrap. She lit the fire, put on some Christmas music and got started.

She'd barely made a dent in the rewrapping when she heard a noise at the door. Had Adam arrived early with Emi?

Had Ian come back for her?

The door opened, and Hope's heart lodged in her throat as a woman strode into the room.

"Hello, Hope. I'd say it's good to see you after all these years, but I doubt you feel the same."

Hope tried to speak, but it was as if a vise had closed around her neck. "Adrianna," she managed to croak. "I thought you—"

Adrianna's laugh chilled her to the bone. "Thought I was dead? That was such a magnificent crash, wasn't it? I was sorry I couldn't wait around to see your friends arrive to investigate."

"But..." Hope's heart thundered in her chest. "Your car. How?"

There was that laugh again. Hope shivered as Adrianna flicked a hand at her.

"You never did watch enough movies. It was just that old brick-on-the-accelerator trick. I don't know if they'll ever figure it out. The car is pretty well toasted."

Hope struggled to focus on Adrianna's voice as reality hit with terrifying force. She was alone in this house with a woman who wanted her dead, and there was no Ian to rescue her this time.

Adam would be arriving with Emi, but the last thing she wanted was for her daughter to arrive to this. Her phone was in her coat pocket on the chair. She couldn't even try to call for help.

"Tsk, tsk. You're thinking too hard, Hope." Adrianna walked across the room and picked up one of the un-wrapped presents. "Is this for Emi? You never did introduce me to your baby girl."

Hearing her daughter's name spoken from such evil lips terrified Hope. Knowing she had to find a way to take charge before Adam arrived with Emi, Hope found her voice. "Why would I have? You were never a part of my life after you left school."

"Was forced to leave, you mean."

The venom dripping from Adrianna's voice left no doubt in Hope's mind that this was all payback. "How long have you been planning this?"

"Since the day Steve had his little chat with the dean. He sounded so convincing. So innocent. As if he'd never had a part in any of it."

"You know he didn't. Steve doesn't play dirty." Hope

had thought to distract Adrianna so she could make a run for the door, but her words had the opposite effect.

"You always did choose men of...honor." Adrianna sneered as she said the last word with such disdain that her smooth veneer cracked. "Speaking of men of honor, one of them will be paying the ultimate price today."

Hope's thoughts immediately flew to Ian, but Adrianna's next words corrected that thought.

"Too bad. Adam has such a nice family." She shrugged. "That's what he gets for playing hero and interfering in my plan."

For the first time Hope understood why guilt haunted Ian. She wasn't really to blame for whatever Adrianna was planning to do to Adam, but if she didn't find a way to stop it, she'd never forgive herself.

"What are you talking about?" Hope needed information so she could figure out a plan.

"Just a little explosion. A roadside accident." She smiled. "Don't worry. He won't feel a thing. It's your pain I want."

"Adam has done nothing to you."

Adrianna shrugged carelessly. "But he's driving your daughter. Your precious little girl. Steve's goddaughter."

Rage such as she'd never known filled Hope. "Leave my daughter out of this." She lunged at Adrianna.

"Not so fast, dear Hope."

Adrianna lifted her arm, and Hope felt the barrel of a gun press into her side.

"Don't push me too far or you won't live to see the grand finale."

Keeping the gun pointed at Hope, Adrianna picked up the remote and powered on the television, then navigated to a streaming channel. She whipped the scarf from around her neck and signaled to Hope to sit in the chair.

"If you cooperate, we'll watch it together," she promised as she bound Hope's arms behind her back and tied them around the back of the chair.

"Watch what?" Hope ground out the words, though her terrified heart already knew the answer.

Adrianna ignored her. "Steve will have to watch the re-play— Oh wait, the hospital will be just as toasted as my car was." She gave another cavalier shrug. "I guess we'll have to enjoy it just the two of us. Too bad I forgot the popcorn."

The snow was picking up, and the easy drive from earlier wasn't as pleasant now. Ian was glad he had Nancy's truck as the wind kicked up and visibility lowered. He punched the button for the heater. It was cold inside too, without Hope's presence to warm his heart.

As he threaded his way through the crowded streets of Christmas Village, Ian replayed their conversations in his mind. Ever since he'd kissed her, his heart had been con-flicted. He was weighted by grief and guilt over his failure to save his wife and child, but was it a life sentence? Hope and Emi had opened his heart in ways he'd never expected, made him feel things he didn't know he was capable of.

Hope had frozen him out after he'd kissed her, but what had he expected? That he could confess his failure as a hus-band and then have a woman whose husband had cheated on her open her arms and risk it happening all over again?

Snow beat against the windshield, but it was nothing compared to his whirling thoughts. Holding Hope in his arms, when she'd thought her world had ended, had shaken something loose in him, reminded him of how very fragile life could be, of what a gift it was. So now he wondered. What if this wasn't how it had to be? What if he could convince Hope that he had changed because of her, that he could acknowledge his mistakes and learn from them rather than wallow in the past?

He laughed sadly. That didn't sound very convincing even to his ears, but could he really just drive away without even trying? Did he really need to abandon a chance for happiness when it would cost hers also? Or was it possible that God was giving him another chance to redeem himself?

Ian wasn't certain of any answer but one—if he didn't go back, if he didn't at least try, he would never know the answers to any of those questions, and for the rest of his life he would regret losing a chance with Hope.

Before his brain could overrule his heart, he swung into a U-turn and headed back to the chalet.

There was a car in the driveway, but Ian didn't think it belonged to Adam. He'd never seen his friend drive anything this sporty. Concern gave way to fear as he tried to call Adam and got an "all circuits busy" response.

Ian drove past the house, pulled over down the street and headed back on foot. If there was trouble inside, which seemed increasingly likely, he didn't want to alert anyone. The front door stood slightly ajar, as if it hadn't been shut tightly and the wind had blown it open. He eased his way up the steps and silently stepped to the side of the door. He could hear the murmur of Hope's voice, and his heart eased, until he heard the clearly spoken response.

"Steve will have to watch the replay." There was a pause and then: "Oh wait, the hospital will be just as toasted as my car was." A longer pause and slight chuckle gave way to "I guess we'll have to enjoy it just the two of us."

The blood started pounding so hard in Ian's ears that he missed anything she said after *us.* That had to be Adrianna.

Somehow his sister's team was wrong. She hadn't died in that crash. She was here to get Hope.

Ian strove for the mental calm he'd learned in the military. He focused his breathing and worked to formulate a plan. Much as he wanted to burst in and rescue Hope, he needed to know what was going on. Thinking first avoided casualties later.

He crept closer to the door and tried to see where Adrianna was. The sight of Hope bound to a chair struck terror in his heart, but at least that meant they weren't planning to go anywhere.

Adrianna was pacing, waving the remote at the television. He ducked just as she started to turn back.

"Adrianna, please," Hope begged. "Think about this. Emi is an innocent child. She has never brought harm to anyone. Your grievance is with me, with Steve. Please don't harm her or Adam."

The raw agony in Hope's plea tore through Ian's heart. He crouched beside the door, and as he tried to strategize, Adrianna's laughter reached him.

"I know," she replied to Hope. "That's why you are going to watch her die. See that outcropping? Keep your eyes focused on that. When Adam's car reaches it, and the bomb detonates, your life will be ruined...like mine was."

Ian's mind struggled to wrap itself around the pure evil that would murder an innocent. Suddenly the "all circuits busy" response made sense. Adrianna must have somehow jammed the signal. They'd underestimated the woman. Clearly the server they'd taken down hadn't been her only resource.

Ian waited until it sounded like Adrianna was facing away again, and he edged forward so he could peer in the opening. He could see the image on the screen, and fury gripped him. He knew exactly where she'd set that bomb, and there was no way Adam would be able to avoid it.

Ian fell to his knees and offered a prayer for guidance. Only God could help him combat such darkness. He knew in his heart what he had to do, but now he needed the courage to execute the difficult choice. He slowly backed away from the door, praying Adrianna wouldn't sense his movement.

Leaving Hope behind was the hardest struggle he'd ever faced, and it almost destroyed him, but as Ian thought about her reaction earlier when she'd thought Emi was dead, he knew it was the only choice. Hope would never forgive him if he chose her over Emi. If he let Emi die to save her life.

When he was a safe distance from the chalet, Ian broke into a run. He hopped in the truck and tried again to reach Adam, but the same "all circuits busy" message came up. His next call was to Nancy.

He breathed a sigh of relief when she came on the line.

"Hey brother. I thought you'd be happy spending time with Hope—"

Ian cut her off. "Adrianna is not dead. She currently has Hope tied to a chair in the chalet and she, or someone who works for her, has planted a bomb on the road Adam is driving."

"I'm putting you on speaker. The team is still here." Nancy's voice reflected the gravity of the situation.

Ian quickly explained what he'd just witnessed. His voice broke as he described leaving Hope. "I can't reach Adam. The circuits are jammed. But I know a shortcut through the mountains. I'm going to try to get there first, detonate it before he arrives. You need to get people to the hospital and clear it. Send another team to the chalet, but don't go in unless she's in imminent danger. Best I can tell, Adrianna plans to make her watch the blast and—" he could barely get the words out "—watch Emi die."

Ian already had the truck in motion by the time Nancy replied. "We'll do exactly that, and we'll keep trying to reach Adam. Keep in touch, Ian. Godspeed. I'm praying for you."

In his mind, Ian mapped the back route to the outcropping. If he pushed the truck as hard as he could, just maybe he could beat Adam to the narrow pass at the outcropping. Snow was falling harder, but he hoped that was to his advantage this time. Adam would drive more slowly given his precious cargo and the treacherous conditions. He glanced at the dashboard clock. Time was running out.

# TWENTY

Hope's eyes were burning from staring at the screen, but she couldn't tear her gaze away. She'd been tied to this chair for close to an hour now, and she'd been unable to come up with any way to stop Adrianna's madness and save her daughter's life. Why had she sent Ian away? If the two of them had been here together, they might have been able to overpower her.

Adrianna had made herself a cup of coffee and paced the room as she drank it, further frazzling Hope's nerves. She'd tried reasoning with her, bargaining with her, pleading for old time's sake, but nothing could get through to her.

Hope gave yet another tug on the silk scarf that bound her, and her heart leaped. This time she felt the material give.

Adrianna swung the gun loosely. "I don't know why you're even bothering to try to get away. It's too late for you to stop it now anyway. Based on his departure time, I'd say Adam should be arriving in about ten minutes now, give or take a little extra time for the weather."

"How can you be so heartless?" Hope cried in desperation. "You are someone's daughter. How would your mother feel if she were the one tied to this chair watching you in danger?"

Adrianna shook her head and gave a chuckle. "Poor example, Hope. My mother, as you may recall, was barely aware of my existence. Having a baby didn't fit into her life plan, so I was exiled to an elderly aunt. But nice try. I'm sure your daughter has been well loved in her short life."

Hope didn't know what to say. She prayed, as she had over and over for these past sixty minutes. And she tugged at the silk again. Because Adrianna was wrong. If she could get loose, she could call Adam and stop him.

She gave a final tug, and the scarf shredded. She waited for Adrianna's attention to turn to the screen again. Hope had noticed that it was the only thing that kept her focused. As Adrianna sipped her coffee and stepped closer to the screen. Hope leaped from her chair and ran for her phone.

Adrianna didn't seem to care. "It won't do any good, you know. I jammed the circuits. You won't get through."

Hope had to try anyway, hoping it was a lie, but a recording announcing "All circuits are busy. Please try your call later," echoed in her ear. She tried the state troopers next but got the same message.

"Ah, here they come now."

Hope didn't want to look, but she couldn't stop herself. She gazed up at the screen and watched the truck she recognized as Adam's slowly enter a deep bend before the narrow pass that would lead to the outcropping. Her heart was in her throat, and tears poured down her cheeks as she prayed over and over again for God to save her little girl.

"What the blazes?" Adrianna exploded in anger. "Who is that? What is he doing?"

Hope squinted at the screen, and the heart she didn't think could bear any more pain shattered all over again. "That's Ian," she whispered as she recognized Nancy's truck.

Ian, her hero, the man she had grown to love in such a short time, was driving his truck right at the outcropping. Somehow he'd discovered Adrianna's plan, and he was sacrificing his life to save Emi's. But it was too late. She couldn't watch.

Hope sank to the floor, her face buried in her hands as she heard the explosion blast through the speakers. She huddled into a ball and sobbed.

"This is the FBI," came a voice over a megaphone. "You are surrounded. Come out with your hands in the air."

Numb, Hope lifted her head. They were too late to save anyone, but if they at least caught Adrianna, she could never cause anyone else such devastation.

Adrianna was so mesmerized by the explosion on the screen that she didn't even seem to register the commands from outside. Trying not to draw her attention, Hope crawled for the door. One glance at the television had told her everything she didn't want to know. She couldn't bear to look at the blazing inferno that was consuming those she loved. All she could hope for was to escape this house so law enforcement could close in on Adrianna.

At the door, she knelt and raised her arms but put a finger to her lips hoping someone understood what she was doing. Once she reached the steps, she got to her feet, kept her hands in the air and ran toward safety.

Sobbing, she explained what had happened and where Adrianna was. A female agent escorted her to a car and offered to let her wait inside, but Hope shook her head. "I have to see her captured." Tears were streaming down her face as she whispered, "She killed the people I most love. I have to see her apprehended."

After what seemed an eternal wait as Hope shivered in the frigid air huddled within a blanket the agent had given her, Adrianna emerged from the house, hands cuffed behind her, escorted by multiple agents.

As they passed by Hope, Adrianna stopped short.

"So many stupid men. So many would-be heroes. What is it about you that inspires such wasted effort?" Adrianna spit the words at her.

Hope forced herself to look at the woman who had destroyed her life. "It isn't anything about me. It's who they are."

She could almost feel sorry for Adrianna that she didn't understand there were people in the world who were heroic by nature, who answered a call for help because they knew no other way to live. Men and woman who were not perfect, but who lived their lives as their Savior taught, people who were truly good at their very core. Men like Ian.

Once they took Adrianna away, Hope slid into the FBI car. She didn't know what she was waiting for, didn't care as time passed in a blur. She had nothing left.

After a while, a vehicle drew up behind her car, sirens blaring and lights flashing. It screeched to a halt, and the door flew open. Hope barely registered the noise until her door opened and she looked up into Nancy's face.

She burst into tears all over again. "I'm so sorry. It's all my fault. If it wasn't for me, Ian would still be alive." Her body convulsed in sobs and shivers.

Nancy nudged her across the seat and climbed in beside her. "What are you talking about?"

"Ian." Hope could barely speak his name. "He tried to save Emi, but they're both dead."

Nancy put a hand on each arm and twisted Hope toward her. "Didn't anyone tell you? They're not dead, Hope. Ian's not dead. Neither is Emi." She made a face. "My truck is toast, but Ian wasn't inside. He pushed it off the ledge into the pass to trigger the bomb. Adam was able to stop in time.

He and Emi are fine." She shook Hope. "Do you hear me? They're alive."

Hope stared at Nancy in disbelief. She knew Nancy wouldn't lie to her, but having heard the explosion and seen the inferno, she was having a hard time wrapping her mind around it.

Nancy pulled her phone from her pocket and sent off a message. "Our tech people are working on restoring service, so fingers crossed this goes through."

Moments later, her phone rang. Nancy opened it, listened and handed the phone to Hope. "It's for you."

Hope accepted the phone gingerly, as if afraid it would explode in her hand. She lifted it to her head. "Hello?"

"Hope, it's me. I love you. Emi's safe. Adam is fine. We did it."

Hope broke into sobs. Her body heaved as it tried to accept his words.

"Hope? Are you there? Do you forgive me?"

Hope breathed deeply. "You're wrong, Ian. *We* didn't do it. *You* did. There's nothing to forgive. And… I love you too," She added in a whisper.

After speaking long enough to assure herself that this was real, and that both Ian and Emi would be coming home to her, Hope got out of the car and handed the phone to Nancy, who had discreetly given her privacy.

"Your brother is pretty amazing." She felt the smile break though her fears.

"I know you love him and all, but please don't tell him that too often. He'll grow unbearable."

Nancy was grinning while she spoke, so Hope laughed, and as the cold air hit her lungs she felt gloriously alive. "I have to warn you, I plan on spoiling him pretty shamelessly."

# TWENTY-ONE

"Mommy, come." Emi tugged at Hope's arm. "I want you to meet my friend Mia."

Hope allowed herself to be pulled along. She was excited too, looking forward to meeting Mia's mom. Though she and Isabelle had spoken several times since Emi returned, they'd yet to meet in person.

The past forty-eight hours had been filled with work as everyone switched their efforts from solving the ransomware attack to preparing the grand finale of Twelve Days 'til Christmas.

Already they'd live streamed from the tree lot and were currently presenting a video on reindeer rescue in preparation for the final two events: harnessing the reindeer to their sleigh for a busy night ahead and Ian's dad doing the traditional Christmas Eve Bible reading beside the fire.

As exciting as it all was though, Hope was ready for it to be over. She and Ian hadn't had a moment alone since Emi had returned, and she was getting more nervous by the minute. Had the words he'd blurted in a moment of euphoria really meant anything?

"Mommy!"

Hope smiled down at Emi. "Yes, dear?"

"You were daydreaming. This is my new friend, Mia, and her mama, Mrs. Isabelle."

Hope knew she was blushing as she looked up at Isabelle, who gave her a wink that hinted she knew exactly who Hope had been daydreaming about.

Hope crouched down to say hello to Mia and thank her for welcoming Emi to her home. Then, as the girls skipped off to watch the reindeer harnessing, she stood and turned to hug Isabelle. "Thank you for coming. Emi's been over the moon to introduce Mia to the reindeer, but I wanted to tell you in person how very much I appreciate you caring for my daughter."

Isabelle smiled and brushed off the thanks. "It wasn't so long ago that I was in your position, accepting help from strangers to protect a child. I was happy to help. It's what friends do, right?" She looked up at Adam, who gazed adoringly back at her before hugging her close.

"Right," he confirmed.

Isabelle glanced over Hope's shoulder and smiled. "We'll get together soon for a playdate and coffee, but why don't Adam and I go gather the reindeer girls and bring them inside? It's almost time for the reading, and I think there's someone here who's waiting for you."

Hope spun around and came face-to-face with Ian. "Hey." She smiled.

"Hey yourself."

As Adam and Isabelle left to get the girls, Ian reached for her hand. "I've missed you. Walk with me back to the house?"

Hope's heart filled as she nodded and clasped his hand in hers.

The ranch family was gathering on the porch and heading into the great room as Hope and Ian arrived. Chairs had been set up in circular rows around the fireplace, and friends and family quickly filled them. Emi and Mia found a place of honor at Poppa's feet, so Ian and Hope hung back, leaning against the wall.

"I know it's a busy night, but I was hoping to spend some time alone with you," he said softly. "Would you meet me after Emi is tucked in bed?"

Hope beamed at him. "She's going to be excited. It might be pretty late."

Ian bent and kissed her lightly. "I'll wait."

At the front of the room, his mother began to softly sing. "Silent night, holy night."

All around the room voices joined in.

Ian kept her hand tucked in his, and Hope let the joy of Christmas wash over her. "All is calm, all is bright."

Poppa's deep bass rang out. "Now all this was done, that it might be fulfilled which was spoken of the Lord by the prophet, saying, Behold, a virgin shall be with child, and shall bring forth a son, and they shall call his name Emmanuel… God with us."

As the service ended, and the tech staff posted a message of love from Steve to end the celebration, the crowd surged toward the table where treats had been spread.

Ian tugged Hope away into a quiet corner. "Penny for your thoughts?"

She stared at the floor and gathered her nerve. "I was thinking that in churches all around the world tonight, people will gather to celebrate the birth of a child who came to bring us forgiveness." She laced her fingers through his and gazed up at him. "Don't you think that if He could be born only to sacrifice and die for us, we can learn from that and forgive one another…and ourselves?"

She held his gaze as his fingers tightened around hers.

"I think we believe in a merciful God, a God of second chances..." He paused as his voice cracked. "A God who could bring two wounded souls together to find forgiveness and healing...and love."

Hours later, when the excitement had finally faded away, when Emi had finally stopped talking about reindeer and fallen asleep, when the house was quiet, Hope made her way down the stairs, praying that Ian was still waiting.

As she came around the turn in the stairs, she saw his tall, muscular frame standing by the window, silhouetted by the lights of the Christmas tree.

She sneaked up behind him and rested her head against his shoulder. "Waiting for someone?"

"Only the love of my life."

He turned, and Hope thought he would kiss her, but he reached for her coat, which lay on the arm of the chair. "You're going to need this."

"We're going somewhere?"

"For a walk in the snow."

She laughed. "I feel like we've done a lot of that."

"This is different. It's Christmas snow." He helped her into her jacket and wrapped a scarf around her neck. After donning his own coat, he led her out the front door.

As they stepped off the porch, Hope lifted her face to the snow. It was gentle, nothing at all like the blizzard that had brought them together.

"Where are we going?"

"It's a surprise." He winked, and her heart melted.

Ian led her around the back of the house and through a stretch of woods. She could see a glow in the distance. Puzzled, she cast a glance at him, but he was giving nothing away.

As they neared the edge of the forest, Ian stopped her. He unwrapped the scarf from her neck and turned it into a blindfold.

"Ian, I can't see."

"That's the point." He laughed. "Do you trust me?"

"With my life," she answered solemnly.

"Then come." He held her hand and led her slowly forward.

Unable to see, Hope focused on her other senses. She felt the tickle of the snow against her forehead, heard the crackling of a fire and smelled the sweet smoke mingling with the scent of evergreens in the fresh cold air. And she felt the security of Ian's hand holding hers.

Finally, he stopped. Standing close beside her, he slowly undid the knot in her scarf. As the wool fell away, Hope gasped. Before her stood a beautiful snow cave alight with Christmas lanterns.

"I built it just for us," Ian whispered as he led her toward the entrance. "For our own private Christmas. It won't last forever," he said, taking her into his arms, "but my love for you will. I want us to build a life together, Hope, a future to share."

Love flooded Hope's heart. She rested in his embrace as she gazed into his beloved face. "I haven't yet had a chance to thank you properly."

He started to speak, but she rested a finger over his lips. "I will thank God every day for the rest of my life for the gift of you, and I am thankful beyond words for everything you have done, have sacrificed for me."

She reached up on tiptoes and rested a hand on either side of his face. "But make no mistake about it, this is not about gratitude." She kissed him lightly. "This is because I love you with all my heart, and more than anything I want to build that life with you…forever." She leaned into his embrace and kissed him with all the love that was overflowing her heart.

\* \* \* \* \*

*If you liked this story from Cate Nolan,
check out her previous
Love Inspired Suspense books,*

Colorado Mountain Kidnapping
Texas Witness Threat
Christmas in Hiding

*Available now from Love Inspired Suspense!
Find more great reads at www.LoveInspired.com.*